CRUEL
SEPTEMBER

DANIEL D. VICTOR

Hardcover ISBN 978-1-80424-317-6
Paperback ISBN 978-1-80424-318-3
ePub 978-1-80424-319-0
PDF 978-1-80424-320-6

Published by MX Publishing
335 Princess Park Manor, Royal Drive, London, N11 3GX
www.mxpublishing.co.uk

Cover design by Brian Belanger

Also by Daniel D. Victor

The Seventh Bullet:
The Further Adventures of Sherlock Holmes

A Study in Synchronicity

Sherlock Holmes and the Shadows of
St Petersburg

The Literary Adventures of Sherlock Holmes,
Volumes 1 and 2

Books in the Series,
"Sherlock Holmes and the American Literati":

The Final Page of Baker Street

Sherlock Holmes and the
Baron of Brede Place

Seventeen Minutes to Baker Street

The Outrage at the Diogenes Club

Sherlock Holmes and the London Particular

The Astounding Murder at Cloverwood House

Sherlock Holmes and the Pandemic of Death

Sherlock Holmes and the Case of the Fateful Arrow

Sherlock Holmes and a Tale of Greed

Acknowledgments

I would like to thank the large number of
people who've helped me with this project
over the years.

(Though not all of them are educators, most
are—
and all of them were taught by teachers.)

For Norma,
Whose strength and sensitivity should serve as
inspiration for us all.

Author's Note

All the characters in this novel are fictional.
Sadly, the same can't be said about the situations in
which they find themselves.

If I ever leave Los Angeles, it will not be because of the traffic, or the city's inability to aid the unhoused, or even the sight of all those celebrity lawns in the middle of a drought. No, the only thing that could force me out of my chosen home of three decades is September. September in Los Angeles is the worst—a culturally manipulative, psychologically abusive, dirty con of a month.

– Mary McNamara
Los Angeles Times

Year One

(September 1969 – June 1970)

Chapter One

Union Business

*T*wo administrators in two days—plenty of reason to be alarmed.

Let me say from the start that we did our best to be discreet. Back then, we were cautious teachers, Mandy and I. Though we met on the first day of school in September of '69, we didn't start dating for a couple of weeks. We spent virtually no time on campus alone together, and we were always sure to go to movies and restaurants far from the Phillips neighborhood. We even drove to school in separate cars on the days such occasions presented themselves.

But that's the thing. It was because we'd been so careful in our social meetings that those back-to-back visits to Mandy's classroom felt so ominous. Sure, Mandy was a brand-new teacher, but it was already November and they'd had plenty of time to see that she was good. She knew her subject; she engaged her students; she controlled her classes. Clearly, there was no need for micro-managing her work.

Skeptics might argue that I was biased about her talents as a teacher since by the time those visits occurred, we'd already been dating a couple of months. But I wasn't the only one offering such praise. In just her second week at Phillips, Mandy's department chair had told her, "You relate to the kids like a veteran."

On the day before the second observation, Mandy had told me about the first, the visit by the principal: how Vivian Laws had appeared in her classroom during period one. How he'd struck his standard pose at the door—short arms folded, stubby legs spread, egg-shaped body swaying forward and back. How he'd stood there for five minutes like a field marshal checking out the room.

At the same time, the kids had been diligently writing an essay on the differences between the Articles of Confederation and the Constitution. Then, the kicker— just before leaving, just when any reasonable person might expect to hear a compliment for their well-behaved class, he'd walked up to Mandy and whispered, "Three students chewing gum."

Now, little more than twenty-four hours later, she'd been paid another visit.

"Who was it this time?" I asked. We were sitting in the faculty cafe at lunch, me with a paper-thin burger, Mandy with the breaded chicken strips she brought to eat every day.

"Mrs. Steele. Third period."

I frowned at the mention of the Girls' Vice-Principal, a born bureaucrat. Though the G.V.P. was mainly responsible for social affairs like the Mother-Daughter Tea and curricular issues like the distribution of books, she was also the primary observer of teachers in their classrooms. "So, how'd it go?"

Mandy's green eyes lit up. "The class was great. We had a lively discussion on the Bill of Rights. The kids were really into it. Then again, maybe it was too much for Mrs. Steele to appreciate. Throughout the lesson, she kept looking around the room. The woman did everything but watch me teach."

"They're good at that," I said and took a bite out of the burger.

"You're right. As soon as the class was over, she pointed to some books I'd stacked on the floor. 'Move those to a closet,' she ordered, like she could hardly wait to tell me, like she'd been holding it in the whole hour. But I'm a reasonable person, and I said I'd put them away."

"What else?"

"Nothing else. She had nothing more to say. That's when I asked her straight out what she thought of my lesson."

"And?"

"All she said was, 'Your blinds are crooked.'"

"Wait," I said. "They're not crooked. They're broken; they don't work."

"That's what I told her, Art, and she said that in that case I should see to it that they're all broken at the same level."

I exhaled loudly.

"Oh, it gets better," Mandy said, eyebrows arched. "After all her complaining, the last thing she told me was that I shouldn't feel so threatened by constructive criticism."

I just shook my head.

"And we're supposed to take these people seriously?"

"That's about right," I said. "This *is* a junior high school, after all."

She set her jaw and pushed away her chicken strips. "Just so you know, it pisses me off."

I first saw Mandy on the pupil-free day before classes began. In retrospect, it seems fitting. To most people, the start of an academic year provides visions of hope, new opportunities, the chance to dream. Following a three-month summer break, the first day of school offers a sense of rejuvenation. At least, it's supposed to.

Lots had gone on in the world since school had ended the previous June. After all, it was the summer of '69. In July, Neil Armstrong had walked on the moon. In August, Jimi Hendrix and company had rocked out at Woodstock. And come September, only a few weeks before school started, Ho Chi Minh had died in North Vietnam.

All of that—and yet to me the new school year still felt pretty much like the old one—same library, same faces, same routine. Even the same L.A. weather. Not much difference between that hot morning in September on the first day of school and those sweltering days that tormented us just before summer break.

Okay, I'm generalizing. Not everything was the same. Before the end of the previous semester, I'd been elected the school's union representative, and at this, our initial faculty meeting, I'd be speaking to my colleagues for the first time in my new position. In fact, it was because I was so intent on composing my inaugural address that I missed seeing any of the new teachers enter the library. Needless to say, that included Mandy.

As most of the chairs were already occupied, she had taken a seat at one of the large tables up front three rows ahead of mine. Her back was to me, so when I finally did look up, all that caught my eye was a fall of long straight hair the color of cinnamon. A moment later, she turned my way, and I could see how she parted it in the middle and how green her eyes were. I figured she was in her early twenties, though the plaid skirt, the light-blue Oxford blouse, and the green-canvas book bag on the table made her look more like a college student than a professional educator.

I could have gone on staring at her a little longer, but right after she'd turned towards me, the heavy-set Corny Whittaker eased herself into a chair at the table between us. Pretty ironic. Corny goes on leave for a year and winds up coming back just in time to block my view. Then again, I figured it was probably for the best. I needed to begin writing the speech I was supposed to be giving later on.

I really did have the noblest of intentions when I picked up my pen. "Unity and brotherhood," I wrote on a sheet of notebook paper, but after thinking about it for a minute I crossed out the words—too political for this faculty. I tried "Prepare for a strike," but crossed those words out as well—too aggressive. What I really wanted was a classic opening—something with educational flare, something insightful. Surely, in a library full of teachers I should be able to find some source of inspiration.

In good faith I proceeded to scan the room, but in truth I found little to inspire. Some people were fanning themselves with folded papers; others were working crossword puzzles in ballpoint pen or doodling cartoons on the meeting's agenda sheet. And all of it accompanied by a soundtrack of chatter and gossip.

"Meet anybody special?" someone asked.

"How are your kids?" somebody else wanted to know.

"Spent the vacation hitching through Europe," another voice said.

At the next table over, two math teachers sat huddled together. They spoke softly, but I was close enough to hear.

"Falstaff got transferred last week," Annie Smith said. "He called in to ask what time today's meeting started, and Annette told him not to bother showing up."

Martha O'Reilly shook her head. "What happened?"

"Too many A's—at least, that's the word. Laws wasn't happy. He got the poor guy sent back to Carnegie—you know, the junior high Mike worked seven years to get out of."

To be fair, there were also a few teachers preparing their lessons. Lois Plank, the French teacher seated a few tables to my left, was filling in the squares of a semester calendar. Next to her, department chair Sam Turner, the only African-American social studies teacher at the school, was riffling through the dog-eared pages of a European history text. And directly across the table from me, the bespectacled Penelope Martinez—her nose yet to be color-streaked from pushing back her glasses with chalk-dusted fingers—was employing a bouquet of red and blue and yellow markers to embellish her lesson plans. Their pages, caught in the glare of the sunlight pouring through the library windows, glowed like a medieval manuscript.

Minutes later, the administrators arrived— the boys' and girls' vice-principals and the head-counselor. A random assortment of muted nods greeted them as they made their way among the various library tables towards the podium. Turning to face the faculty, the three settled into the metal folding chairs positioned just to the right of the library's solitary, rotating floor-fan.

I shot another look in the direction of the new teacher, but I couldn't see around Corny. Just as well. I still hadn't written anything useful for my speech. I chewed on my pen a moment, and then in big letters I scrawled, "WELCOME BACK" across the page. I stared at the greeting, considered the sentiment, and congratulated myself on the simplicity of the phrase. People would be expecting some kind of activist oratory from me, and instead I'd be offering a direct, friendly greeting. Fucking brilliant!

Suddenly, everything stopped. No whispering, no doodling, no waving of papers to keep cool. Except for the slow oscillation of the fan, no movement at all. Just everyone looking up front. For behind the podium, clutching a pad of yellow legal paper and surveying the group, stood Vivian Laws.

There were few straight lines about the man. In spite of the heat, he wore a limp, brown sports coat. Between its expansive lapels only his wide, old-fashioned tie—on this day a bright, solid green— had a sharpness. Like a fat emerald arrow, the broad apron pointed halfway down the ample bib of his white shirt, at—but well short of—the two crossed rifles you could discern etched into the solid-brass buckle of his narrow, white belt. As for his olive trousers, where there should have been keen-edged pleats, there were simply blunt, rounded folds.

Upon seeing the principal for the first time, you scarcely realized that he was missing the little finger of his right hand. Mandy told me she hadn't noticed it when she first met him, and I hadn't either. Yet everyone who'd worked at Phillips a while knew about it, and people invented various explanations to account for the finger's absence. Some speculated that Laws had lost it in a heroic battle during World War II. Others suggested something more mundane like a car accident. A particularly wild theory held that some maniacal kid had bitten it off.

To give him his due, Vivian Laws knew how to work a room, prolonging the hush for a few tense moments before carefully placing his yellow pad on the podium. Then with both arms resting on the inclined top, he would sway forward and blow hard into the stationary microphone, an amplified roar exploding from the speaker.

"Testing," Laws thundered. "One-two-three. Testing. Can you hear me?" No one in the library could miss the overpowering sweep of his amplified voice, and yet Laws directed his question to those seated directly before him. Which is why—at least, according to Jack Pointer, my predecessor as union rep—for the seven years Laws had been principal, the faculty had learned to fill up the library from the rear. Let the late-comers serve as the principal's targets.

Though somebody up front nodded that Laws was coming in loud and clear, the principal repeated his counting anyway. Only after a few others agreed that they too could hear him did he put a hand on the side of the mic as if to begin speaking. And yet he continued to stand silently and allow the tension to grow.

At last, when people looked like that they'd had enough, he offered a quick smile, moistened his lips, and glanced down at his notes. "I want to welcome you back." (So much for that idea, I said to myself, scribbling out the very same words on the paper before me.) "Like every vacation," he added, "all good things must come to an end. Now it's time to get to work. Let me start by welcoming back Cornelia Whittaker, who's returning from sabbatical."

The faculty applauded politely as the large, middle-aged woman at the table in front of me rose with an embarrassed wave. She took a step to the side in order to turn and smile, and when she did, I was able to catch a glimpse of the new teacher looking vaguely in my direction.

"I'm on a diet," Corny said softly, tugging at the hem of her tight green blouse. "I'll be fifty pounds lighter by the end of the year."

"Fat chance," quipped Don Frick, the woodshop teacher.

People near enough to hear him shook their heads. At the same time, Corny sat down, and the new teacher disappeared.

"Now," Laws announced, scanning his notes, "it's time to introduce the most recent additions to the faculty."

There were three people joining the staff that fall. The first two stood when Laws called their names—a short and bespectacled second-year math teacher and a tall and grey cooking teacher. Half-hearted clapping welcomed them into the fold. The young woman with the red hair came next. "Amanda Sayer," he called her. She was a social studies teacher, and she was just starting out.

"We won Miss Sayer away from Thomas Paine," Laws said. "She interviewed there as well."

Leaning far to my left, I managed to see Mandy rise from her seat to the sound of more scattered applause. She looked nice enough. I was already considering how to approach her after the meeting.

With the arrival at the podium of the Girls' Vice-Principal, however, such plans seemed far off. This morning, Mrs. LaVerne Steele, a Black woman who'd served with the school district for many years, presented a dramatic image. She sported a golden scarf atop her head, large hoop earrings, and a scarlet-colored skirt that billowed as she walked. It was no secret to all who knew her that the very next day, with students around and Laws on patrol, she would dress much more conservatively.

As Mrs. Steele did at every first meeting, she eased into her speech on the use and care of textbooks. Too bad I couldn't tell the new teachers what a waste of time the vice-principal's pronouncements were since printed copies of the very same information would be placed in our mailboxes later that afternoon.

Mrs. Steele was only the first of the speakers. Next on the agenda was Roland Swett, the Boys' Vice-Principal. In spite of the cloying heat, the short, greying sixty-year-old wore his trademark navy-blue cardigan. As usual, he sported a plaid bowtie and, pinned to his shirt, the round, white badge with the word *SPIRIT* splayed across it in bold, dark-blue letters that matched his sweater.

The administrative job of the B.V.P. was to oversee the school's male-oriented affairs. Although he mainly talked about sports, this day's topic turned out to be another one of his favorites, student discipline. Swett liked to brag that the no-touching rule—his directive that boys keep at least one inch away from one another; girls, two inches; and boys and girls, three—was his own creation. Its recitation never failed to evoke smirks and giggles from the faculty. In fact, when he got to the part about using your thumb (tip to knuckle) as the measure for an inch, half the audience—accompanied by a chorus of laughter—dutifully jerked their thumbs in the air like a large group of umpires making the out-call.

Swett may have missed the sarcasm, but Vivian Laws did not. Standing just behind the vice-principal, Laws aimed his severest glances at the unfortunate teachers seated right in front of him. However limited, it was an effective strategy, for the exuberance that had momentarily lit up the room immediately extinguished itself.

The next administrator up was Abe Norovsky, the head-counselor with the shaggy brown hair and grizzled goatee. He managed to consume a good ten minutes detailing the procedures for the distribution of the kids' class schedules—just as we'd done the year before.

By the time Norovsky handed the mic back to the principal, the large, round clock above the librarian's desk showed 10:30. I still hadn't composed my union speech, and yet there was no need to panic—Laws's morning meetings generally lasted till eleven. Though students were arriving the next day and we could all use the extra time to set up our classrooms, I was confident that Laws wasn't about to let us go early, not with an extra thirty minutes left in front of an audience to whom he could expound his educational philosophy. He didn't let me down.

"Let me begin the school year with a warning," Laws said. "Don't underestimate me. I know that some of you resent my tactics, that a few of you even consider me cold-hearted. But let me remind you people who feel that way, you just don't understand where my great respect for authority comes from."

We did understand, of course, because we'd heard it so often before.

"Oh, I know," Laws said, "some of you think it goes back to my days in the military, and you wouldn't be wrong. That's where I learned the importance of discipline." He seemed to stand a little taller on speaking the word. "But let me tell you that I learned the importance of authority one terrible day some twenty years ago when I was still a teacher."

"The airplane story," Frick whispered.

The Phillips faculty had heard the unhappy tale numerous times, but nobody moved.

"Some of you may recall the horrific mid-air collision of two small planes in the skies above a junior high all those years ago. It was in the east San Fernando Valley, and as one of the teachers there on that awful day, ladies and gentlemen—"

"I understood the need for order," Frick whispered.

"—I understood the need for order," Laws said. "Large chunks of airplane came crashing down onto the playground. Most students were in the building, but there was still a group just finishing P.E.; and while the results could have been much worse, they were bad enough: three boys killed. Only by the grace of God—and because so many students listened to us—did we get lots of others out of harm's way. That's the power of authority. Unless you've seen what I've seen, you can't possibly understand how much strict discipline equates not only with learning, but also with the ability to survive."

Mrs. Nichols, the gray-haired librarian who was seated at the library's main desk, hiccupped a sob.

Laws was on a roll now, employing his favorite tropes. He told us how we were his sheep and he was our shepherd and how he didn't want us following his rules because he told us to but because deep inside, we knew they were right.

Just then Corny shifted her chair to the side so that Amanda Sayer appeared in front of me. A window of opportunity. Hoping the new teacher would look my way, I prepared to smile. Or wave. Maybe—

Suddenly, I heard the principal mention my name. "Although Mr. Malamud doesn't know it yet, I'm asking him to head the Unity Crusade for us this year. As the new union representative, he should relish the opportunity."

"Shit," I said to myself, thoughts of my speech evaporating as I took in Laws's plan. The Unity Crusade may have been a union-endorsed charity, but the principal had told me nothing about setting it up.

"I'm certain Mr. Malamud won't mind filling your mailboxes with Crusade material," Laws said. "He'll put the brochures in your boxes tomorrow morning and collect the money from you for the next few days." He looked in my direction. "Time to muster some enthusiasm, Art. Come up here and say a few words."

Clearly, I had no choice. Worse, no sooner did I get to my feet than the rumblings began; the faculty knew they were about to be asked for money.

"Can't we go to our classrooms?" someone said. Other cries echoed agreement.

Vivian Laws had a way of narrowing his eyes when he smiled that made him look like he was totaling up a bill you owed him. In this instance, his indulgent grin looked triumphant. Worse, he had every reason to feel that way. He could have gotten a clerk in the office to stuff the teachers' mailboxes and collect the donations, but by coercing the union rep—me—into doing the charity work, he'd managed to override any political issues I might have wanted to bring up.

As I wove my way between the tables to the podium, I had plenty of time to appreciate the fix I was in. In addition to having no union speech, I also had nothing to say about the Unity Crusade. Oh, once I got to the mic, I did manage to mutter something about the importance of donating; but the emptier the words I offered up, the greater the number of people I could count staring at the clock or whispering to their neighbors or yawning wide-mouthed in my face. You didn't have to be an expert in crowd control to know that this wasn't the time to be whipping up any union fervor.

"I'll talk politics next time," I reassured myself and, heart racing, signaled for Laws to end the meeting.

No sooner did he announce, "You're all dismissed," than chairs raked the floor and talk filled the air. Classroom preparation beckoned; and gathering up their books and bags, teachers headed for the library's now-open double-doors.

Thanks to her red hair, it was easy to spot the new teacher joining the throng. As I watched her disappear into the hallway, a single sliver of hope crossed my mind—she didn't know I was planning to give a political speech, and so she couldn't possibly have realized how badly I'd just screwed up my first attempt to represent the teachers' union.

Chapter Two

Early Encounters

Jack Pointer had served the teachers' union at Phillips for so many years that everyone called him "Union Jack." That's why the entire faculty was shocked the previous April when he'd taken himself out of the action. "Two years from retirement," he'd said at a sparsely attended union meeting. "Time for someone else to take over."

I, for one, had no interest in replacing him. I'd been teaching just short of three years when he announced his plans, and I had little desire to get involved with union politics. Working with kids provided enough engagement for me. Since the outside world had a way of invading one's usual lessons anyway, as far as I was concerned, encompassing it all required full-time commitment. Talking kids through the assassinations of Martin Luther King and Bobby Kennedy made me appreciate all the more how a teacher needed to focus on the classroom. Kids deserved explanations, guidance, comfort. Compared to those concerns, union affairs seemed trivial.

Jack, however, didn't buy my reasoning. That I'd been at UC Berkeley in '64 during the Free Speech Movement was all he needed to know. To him, I just had to be a political ally.

It wasn't that simple, of course. I'd sat out most of the demonstrations at Cal. You could get put on probation or even kicked out for such disruptive behavior. My parents were paying for my education, and I convinced myself that I shouldn't risk squandering their money.

I certainly hadn't gone to Berkeley to participate in political actions. Born and raised in Los Angeles, all I knew was that the university had an excellent academic reputation and a beautiful bell tower called the Campanile. I'd heard nothing about the social activism in Northern California—nothing about the left-wing demonstrations in San Francisco or the rumors of Communist spies on the Berkeley campus from as long ago as the Manhattan Project; not even anything about the anti-establishment attitude associated with the university's student body in general. To tell the truth, when I applied to Cal in 1962, I had never even heard of the university's nickname, "Berserkeley," supposedly coined a few years earlier by Herb Caen in the *San Francisco Chronicle*.

Let me put it another way: when I started at Berkeley, some character with long hair and a beard looked distinctive enough to be nicknamed "Jesus." By the time I graduated, virtually every guy at Cal—

with the exception of the jocks and the frat rats—looked that way, including me.

I will admit that I cut class to protest the Vietnam War. But that was after the anti-war movement had heated up, and it was pretty common all over campus to hear chants of "Hey, hey, LBJ, how many kids did you kill today?" As long as I wasn't burning my draft card—and threatening my student deferment—I could protest the war in anonymity.

Serving as the union's point man at Phillips was another matter. Although I would have tenure by then and be relatively safe, antagonizing one's principal (one's boss) still seemed more dangerous than protesting anonymously in college—especially when the boss in question seemed so dismissive of his employees. I didn't want to stick my neck out and risk losing my job. Back then, I was thinking only of myself. To my great sorrow, the idea that serving as union rep could result in wounding someone close to me never crossed my mind.

"Can't you get somebody else?" I asked Jack in the late April afternoon when he had encouraged me to take his place. I remember the scene precisely. We were on our way to the parking lot and had just passed the stately birds of paradise that line the pathway from the school to the sidewalk.

Jack arched his tufted eyebrows and rubbed his hand over his bald head. "Whom do you have in mind? Are we not talking about our trusted colleagues who never utter a peep against Vivian Laws at faculty meetings?"

A pair of wrought-iron lampposts stand like sentinels at the end of the path, and Jack continued listening to my protests as we turned past them and headed down the street to the school parking lot. By the time we reached his dusty, blue Ford Galaxie, it was clear that he would not cave. Then again, neither would I.

A week later at lunch, he tried again. "The job's only what you make it," he said, waving his soup spoon in my direction. "No one's going to tell you how much union business you have to do. If doing the minimum will make you happy, just collect the union mail and distribute their flyers. That's it."

I had to hand it to the guy. He saw what I was trying to ignore—that deep down inside, I too believed in all that altruistic propaganda—righting wrongs, defending the downtrodden, educating the masses—concepts I'd grown up believing in, concepts I'd overlooked at Cal to avoid getting sucked into the Free Speech Movement. Union Jack had sniffed out my liberal guilt.

In the end I took the man at his word. It couldn't be that much extra work. It couldn't cost that much extra time. My failure to get involved back in Berkeley still haunted me; Jack was offering the opportunity for another chance, and I agreed to run.

Victory was a formality. I had run unopposed.

My failure to deliver any semblance of a union speech at that first meeting bothered me. What kind of rep was I going to be? What kind of leadership was I displaying? On the other hand, I also had a new semester of teaching to prepare for, and the first order of business was setting up my classroom. To that end, I collected a stack of bright-yellow construction paper from the supplies-closet in the English office and made the familiar trek down the hallway to my room.

Closed up for the summer and devoid of kids, the room felt pristine. The blond, Formica-topped student desks stood in five straight rows of eight; the shiny floor reflected the sunlight, and you could still smell a hint of furniture polish and floor wax. The halcyon scene lasted only a moment though for just after I had entered, Betty Warden, the middle-aged flower child, whose classroom was next to mine, walked in.

She was wearing a baggy, tie-dyed dress featuring jagged circles of blue and red; and beneath her short, platinum hair, her wide eyes and pink face seemed full of excitement. "She wants to meet you," Betty confided.

I first met Betty doing supervision in the hallway at the start of school on my first day of teaching. Our classroom doors were close to each other, and she was quietly singing the Jefferson

Airplane song about Alice and the pills that make you larger and smaller. Closing her eyes, she'd begun to sway.

"Flake," I remember thinking. Out loud, I said, "Listen, I need to get to my class."

"Me too," she said. "But I want to be neighborly and introduce myself." After telling me her name, she added, "I'm forty-six; divorced, have two kids in college, both of whom I drove up to San Francisco last spring, so we could all be together to protest the war."

I had half-expected her to tell me she'd driven them to Berkeley to defend free speech. Still, as much as she bugged me, I came to realize that all she really wanted was to be my best friend. Back in the present, I accepted her enthusiasm in the spirit of camaraderie.

"Who wants to meet me?" I asked. "What are you—"

She cut me off with the crack of her gum. "The new social studies teacher," she said, pulling at the short sleeve of her tie-dyed costume. The dress was expansive and reached down to the floor. "The one with the red hair."

"Come on," I said, "she doesn't even know who I am."

Betty giggled and cracked her gum once more. "Don't worry. We left the library together, and I told her all about you."

I rolled my eyes. "That's all I need."

"Her room's just down the hall," Betty said. "You can thank me later," she added as she turned to enter her own room.

The routine of setting things up helped move the political and social thoughts out of my head. I began by stapling the yellow construction paper over the two walls of pockmarked bulletin boards. On top of all the yellow, I posted the kind of stuff that English teachers accumulate over the years—a map of England, caricatures of famous writers, a chart of diacritical marks, and grammar guidelines on subject-verb agreement and punctuation.

Up to a point, the work did succeed in distracting me, but I must confess that intriguing images of the new red-headed teacher also helped. It was those visions, along with the encouragement I'd gotten from Betty that gave me the impetus. If the new teacher really did want to meet me, maybe she'd join me for lunch.

Mandy's room turned out to be across the hall from the library. "Give it a shot," I told myself; and opening the door, I walked in.

Amanda Sayer was seated at her desk in the process of pulling out some books from her green canvas bag that was lying on the floor near her feet. Her forehead glistened with sweat as she sighed, "So many books."

I smiled in commiseration as she placed a dictionary, thesaurus, and *Encyclopedia of American History* between two black, metal bookends on her desktop.

"Hi," I said. "I'm Art Malamud."

She arched her eyebrows and gave me her full attention. "Not *the* Art Malamud. Not the Art Malamud I've been hearing so much about from Betty Warden."

You couldn't miss the exaggeration. I wanted to laugh, but it came out more of a snort. "Don't believe everything you hear from Betty."

"Oh, I won't. I haven't."

"You're Amanda Sayer," I ventured. "I saw you at the meeting."

"Oh, yeah. You're the guy who talked about the charity. I'm afraid I didn't pay much attention." She paused a moment to run a hand through her red hair, then added, "Everything's so new and all."

"Well, next time I hope to be more noticeable. I'm the union rep here, and I blew my chance to talk about working conditions." Thirty seconds in, and I'd already admitted my latest flaw.

"Betty told me you worked for the union," Amanda said. "But I have to tell you that I'm not much interested in school politics."

"But aren't you a history teacher? Isn't politics what your subject is all about?"

She bristled. "Don't tell me you came in here to sign me up."

Sad to say, the thought hadn't crossed my mind. I did note her defensiveness, but all I said was, "Not really." A thick U.S. history book lay on the desk next to me, and I began fidgeting with its red, white, and blue cover.

"I'm sorry," she said. "This is my first job, it's hot, and I've only just gotten started in here." She swept her arm around the room to indicate the enormity of her task.

I didn't get her complaints. Compared to my classroom, hers looked student-ready. She'd already papered her bulletin boards in orange and beige, and on top of the colored paper she'd stapled a rainbow of historical maps. I recognized the Roman Empire in yellow, the British Commonwealth in pink, the major battles of the American Civil War in greens and browns.

But it was what she'd mounted between the maps that really caught my eye—a set of large, fine-lined drawings, the kind of original work you don't usually see tacked up on classroom bulletin boards. One depicted the White House; another, the Capitol. Others portrayed places I didn't recognize; but thanks to their massive columns and imposing domes, they looked equally important. As I leaned in to examine the inked drawings more closely, I noted the signature "A. Sayer" scripted in tiny letters at the bottom of each one.

"Did you do these?"

"I did," she smiled proudly. "I've always liked drawing buildings."

I stepped back and took another few moments to study the graceful lines and intricate shadings. "These are really good." Then I surveyed the entire room. "Everything in here looks great." I sensed my opportunity. It wasn't exactly like asking her on a date, but it sure felt like it. In any case, I took the chance. "How about a break? What I really came by for is to ask if you want to join me for lunch."

"Join you for lunch?"

"In the faculty cafeteria—you know, with everybody else."

She furrowed her brow; then, reaching into her canvas bag, she produced a brown paper sack. "Sorry," she said, "I brought my own. And I've still got more work to do in here."

"Yeah, okay," I said, unable to decide if I was more annoyed with Betty for whatever she'd told the new teacher about me or with myself for my lame approach. I'd only just met the woman, and she was facing a brand-new job. Perhaps inviting her for lunch had been a bit much.

"Maybe some other time though," she added quickly with what I took to be an encouraging smile.

"I'd like that," I said and feeling a little better, waved good-bye. I shuffled off down the main stairway and exited into the quad.

The hot air hit me as soon as I stepped outside. It served to rekindle the irritation I felt from my overly aggressive come-on. "Give it a rest," I said to myself. "She's got lots on her mind. Don't take it personally. She's new to all this. Tomorrow's the first day of classes."

As I made my way to the cafeteria, I found myself remembering my own first day of teaching.

Chapter Three

In the Beginning

In 1969 I lived in a small, one-bedroom apartment near Robertson just south of Olympic. Situated atop a detached garage, my place stood in the shadows of a much larger apartment building, a pink four-plex with two French-Normandy-style turrets. Both buildings were owned by Mrs. Gross. She lived in the front building and functioned as landlady as well as owner.

Next to the metal stairs leading up to my door stood a crabapple tree. Even though the small green apples were no bigger than golf balls and had a tart, sour taste, I liked the symbolism—an apple for the teacher—especially noteworthy on the first day of school.

Usually I teach in jeans, but every opening day with the kids I always show up in more formal attire, clean-shaven, and hair cut. "Positive antecedent ethos," one of my education professors called it. "Good first impression" made more sense to me.

In any case, when I walked into the main office that first day of classes in 1969 wearing my navy-blue suit; white, button-down shirt; and blue-and-gold, thin-striped tie, I felt prepared for whatever the education gods had in store. In point of fact, I had purposely arrived early enough to complete the first of my tasks, the charity work Laws had foisted upon me during the faculty meeting the day before.

On the back wall of the office above Annette Avalon's desk hung a portrait of David Graham Phillips, the American writer for whom the school had been named. I knew little about him except that around the turn of the century, he'd been a famous journalist and best-selling novelist—not that anyone (besides the people in the school bearing his name) had ever heard of him in the 1960s.

The photograph itself was large, and the dust and sepia tint gave an antique quality to the humorless face posed above an old-fashioned celluloid collar. Phillips' piercing eyes appeared very much alive, however, and it was in the glare of that riveting gaze that I thrust the charity brochures Annette handed me into the alphabetically-arranged, wooden pigeon-holes that served as faculty mailboxes.

It didn't take long for the rest of the teachers to start arriving. They'd initial the sign-in sheet at the counter, retrieve their mail, and head for their classrooms. A few nodded or smiled in my direction as they reached around me to empty their boxes, and every so often someone would complain about the heat or even offer me a greeting.

"Don't worry, good buddy," Don Frick said with a slap on my back. "Lots of success stories start in the mailroom."

It was when I'd reached the W's that my right arm got bumped. Hard. I turned to see Amanda Sayer. She was dressed professionally in brown blazer and matching skirt. Her long red hair was rolled into a bun.

"Oh, did I hit you?" she asked, green eyes wide in surprise. Her tone was exaggerated enough so that it was obvious she'd knocked into me on purpose.

"Sorry," she grinned before I could say a word.

"I hope everything goes well today, Amanda," I smiled back.

"Thanks," she said. "Same to you."

For a moment I thought I might ask her for lunch again, but I caught sight of the brown paper sack peeking out of her book bag. Even though she was the one who'd made contact with me that morning, I stopped myself.

I'm guessing she surmised my friendly intentions. At least, that's how I interpreted her parting words. "Call me 'Mandy,'" she said with a sympathetic smile and after making a quick turn, hurried out of the office.

🎓

In the five straight rows of eight desks, some forty eighth-graders sat before me. Forty people. (It always sounds like more when you call students "people.") Although I'm sure that many of them had butterflies dancing in their stomachs on that first day of school, I don't imagine any of them considered how such anxieties might also be plaguing their teachers. All kinds of bad things can happen on the first day of class. Mispronounce someone's name that all the other kids already know, leave a shoelace untied, get something caught between your teeth— and you're forever labeled a dork (or worse).

That's why I always stuck to the same routine on opening-days. I would begin each of my classes with a description of what we were going to study that semester—classic novels like *Treasure Island,* for instance, or broader subjects like Greek mythology. Then I'd announce that I'd be assigning essays on the literary topics we covered in class as well as on the books the kids read on their own.

I explained bureaucratic procedures like attendance, make-up assignments, and book distribution—how they'd get a grammar text for the entire semester but novels and anthologies only when the schedule called for them. In addition to the mechanics of getting things done, I always saved a few minutes at the end to speak about my philosophy of teaching English: how I view grammar, composition, and literature as integrated elements and how you can't talk about one without dealing with the other two.

All went well for me that first day, and I assumed they did in Mandy's classes too, for on the second day she took her hair out of the bun; and on Friday of the first week, though she still had brought her brown paper bag to school, she joined Jack, Betty, and me at lunch in the teachers' cafeteria.

After school on Tuesday of the second week, Mandy also sat with us at the faculty meeting.

"Right on schedule," Jack said. "Two weeks, two meetings. Teachers get paid until 3:00; principals, until 4:30. That's all you need to know."

The purpose of the meeting was to enable Abe Norovsky to explain the procedures for "permanent-program day"—the date (still two weeks away) when students were formally signed into their new classes. Since the number of teachers allotted to a school was based on the number of students officially enrolled, the process took on added significance. If the count was down far enough, teachers would lose their jobs.

Once Norovsky had finished, Laws commandeered the microphone.

The topic was student dress, and Laws proceeded to make his usual points—how young people should come to school properly groomed, how he wanted "to see undergarments" if someone tore their clothes, and how it was the teacher's job "to protect girls from themselves" when they wore something you could see through, especially in hot weather.

Mandy let out a deep breath. "He can't be serious."

As if he'd heard her, Laws threatened unsatisfactory notices to teachers who ignored such violations. And for good measure, he warned the women on the faculty not to shorten their skirts by rolling them up.

"The sexual revolution is not coming to Phillips Junior High School," Laws declared.

Then he allowed his voice to trail off. He seemed to sense that his audience might be drifting away. That's when he called on me.

This time I was ready; I had prepared in advance. "In unity there is strength," I addressed the faculty—trite, to be sure, but truthful nonetheless. I went on to offer a few words about union membership and the importance of group solidarity, and I even received some applause for my efforts. At the end, I announced that I'd heard nothing new concerning the recurrent hints of a teachers' strike, and to placate Laws, I plugged the Unity Crusade. By the time we left the library, I was feeling proud of my presentation.

"So, what do you think of Laws's little empire?" Jack asked Mandy as we exited the school. Though it was late in the afternoon, the September sun still shone fiercely, and the red-brick building cast a long, narrow shadow.

Mandy shrugged. "To be honest, I figure most principals are like him. Even so, I was surprised that nobody complained about all that dress-code nonsense, especially the part about the teachers. Actually, it gives me the creeps."

"I hear you," Jack said.

"I can't be the only person it bothered," Mandy said. She tapped me on the arm as we turned onto the sidewalk. "You're the union rep, Art. Aren't you the one who's supposed to be speaking up for all of us? Aren't you the one who's supposed to be complaining?"

Besides the word "yes," I didn't have a good answer, and so I said nothing.

We remained silent until we reached the parking lot. It was then that Mandy turned to Jack. "If these rules bother you so much," she asked him, "how have you managed to survive for so many years?"

"Me?" he said, jingling his car keys as he approached the blue Galaxie. "Easy. I consider it all a circus. If I come to school every day expecting to laugh at the clowns, I'm never disappointed." With a wink at both of us, he added, "Or surprised."

Jack unlocked his car, slid in behind the wheel, and slammed the door shut. Rolling down the window, he offered a quick little wave. "Don't misunderstand me," he said before turning the key, "when I say 'clowns,' I'm not talking about the

42

kids." Then he fired up the engine, backed the Galaxie out of its spot, and rumbled off towards the open gate at the driveway.

The old Ford disappeared down the street, and Mandy and I stood there staring at each other in the heat. With the sun in my face, I had to squint.

"From what I've seen around here," Mandy said, "I think Jack's got the right idea."

I mumbled something in agreement, and then we were just standing there staring at each other again, neither one of us making a move to leave. Maybe it was the heat that prompted me. In any case, shading my eyes so I could see her response, I dared to ask, "Want to go out for dinner?"

"Sure," she grinned. "Why not?"

Chapter Four

A Couple

*T*hat evening marked the official beginning of our relationship. Mandy suggested we eat near her place on the West Side so she could avoid getting home too late after dinner.

"Lesson plans to do," she said.

I suggested The Fox and Hounds in Santa Monica. Since neither one of us wanted to return to Phillips after dinner to pick up our cars, we decided to drive separately—Mandy in her lotus-white VW Beetle and me in my light-green Dodge Dart, the model famous for its push-button automatic transmission.

We met in the parking lot, and Mandy pointed to the wooden beams and modest gables of the restaurant. "Tudor Revival," she said, "It looks like fun."

I thought so. I especially loved the dark, lead-glass windows; the rosewood paneling; the redbrick fireplace; and the deep, brown-leather wing chairs. The prime rib was good too.

Dinner progressed smoothly—so smoothly that once we'd finished our coffees, Mandy invited me back to her apartment. A good sign, I thought. It wasn't far, she said; and minutes later, I was eagerly driving down Olympic to Bundy behind her VW.

Just north of the intersection, we entered a driveway on Bundy that opened into a narrow parking lot. To the left stood a line of leafy magnolias, and in the lingering twilight I could see beyond them a string of attached, single-level apartments, their terracotta roof tiles qualifying them as Spanish-style—at least, in L.A.

When Mandy reached the center of the drive, she turned left and parked in front of the trees. I pulled in next to her, and amidst the sweet smell of jasmine we headed off between the magnolias for the row of small apartments. Mandy's was in the middle and had a white façade and a black front door. But then so did all the rest of them.

Inside, I felt like I was back in college. A cane lamp perched on an old orange crate lit up the place. There were rickety bookshelves made of unpainted wooden planks and weathered cinder blocks; a wooden rocker with blue cushions faced an old couch of burgundy-colored corduroy, its white stuffing poking out at the corners like fresh popcorn, a bright-orange velour pillow leaning against an arm. Various plants—hanging spiders, potted succulents, and a climbing Pothos—provided splashes of green.

But as in her classroom, what most caught my attention was a pair of delicate architectural drawings mounted on the wall, each an icon of the New York skyline. One depicted the Art Deco lines of the

Chrysler Building and the other, the tapering spire of the Empire State. Both were done in black ink and featured various shadings of yellow, brown, red, and blue. Like the ones I'd seen at Phillips, the lower-right corners bore the signature, "A. Sayer."

"These are really good," I told her.

"Thanks," she blushed. "It's sort of a hobby—drawing, I mean. Architecture has always fascinated me, you know, growing up in New York and all. When I was three, my parents took me to the Empire State Building. As soon as I got home, I drew a picture of it with crayons—or so they told me." She nodded at the more recent version on the wall. "I've been doing it ever since."

"How about some music?" she said, and from a nearby shelf pulled out a Simon and Garfunkel album. Moments later, speakers in the corners of the room offered up the short guitar riff that opens "The Sound of Silence." With the familiar voices of crystal harmony in the background, we sat down on the couch, and she told me her recent life history— how her mother had died when Mandy was still in high school, how her dad was a lawyer in Manhattan, and how she ended up going to college in Central New York so she could stay relatively close to home in case her father needed her.

"What school?" I asked.

"Ithaca. Have you heard of it?"

"The home of Odysseus."

"Not the same place," she laughed, "though I assure you that anybody who's gone to school there knows all about Homer. It's a beautiful campus—lakes, waterfalls, gorges. I've sketched many a landscape there."

"I can only imagine."

"In the end," she said, "I came to L.A. for work because the job market for teachers seemed so good."

"Me too." I told Mandy about growing up in L.A., how I'd gone to Cal, and how my parents had retired to Miami Beach.

"I thought about going to Berkeley," she said, "in my senior year of high school. The architect Julia Morgan went there, so you know it's a great school, and I loved the pictures I saw of the campus." A shadow crossed her face "But it was so far away with my mom being sick. Besides, my dad didn't want me going there in the first place—because of the riots."

Here we go again, I thought. I hadn't been back to Berkeley in more than five years, and yet I was still having to defend my alma mater. I could feel my face turning red. "Just so you know," I said, "there weren't any riots."

"Tell it to my dad."

"Talking about riots, after the one here in Watts in '65, teachers were hard to come by. People didn't want to move to L.A. In fact, when I interviewed for jobs a year later, some recruiter in the district office asked me if I was even willing to teach the 'culturally disadvantaged children of the curfew area'—that's what they called the kids of color living in Watts. Once I told them I'd teach anywhere, they were more than happy to send me out on interviews."

"How'd you end up at Phillips?" Mandy asked.

"Actually, I started out looking for a job in a high school. Silly me, I thought I'd be teaching sophisticated literature to mature young people. It didn't take long into my job-search to give up that idea. I'd shaved my beard and cut my hair, but even so the high-school principals who interviewed me were less interested in what I wanted to teach than the fact that I'd graduated from 'Berserkeley.'

"'No political missionaries need apply,' one told me. Another one said, 'I know you Berkeley types. And I don't want anybody on my faculty shacking up all night and then come dragging his weary ass in here in the morning.' So much for high schools."

"That's terrible," Mandy said.

"Tell me about it. Anyway, that's how I ended up at a junior high. Actually, Phillips isn't so bad—if you can ignore the principal. Besides I needed the job. There's a war going on, and I didn't want to get drafted. Still don't."

The first side of the album came to an end, and Mandy got up to flip the disc. As "Richard Cory" started up, she asked, "So how come you haven't been? Drafted, I mean."

"Sheer luck." The luckiest day of my life, actually. Back in '62, I'd gone to buy some jeans at the Sears near Santa Monica and Western. Just down the street I saw a Selective Service office. I was eighteen and had to register for the draft, and back then there was no war going on in Vietnam—not an American war, anyway. The office was right there— simple—so I decided that instead of waiting until I went off to college, I'd go in right then to register. There was no line or anything. It seemed easy enough."

"So where was the luck?"

"Well, I hadn't really thought about how far east I'd driven. There were lots of guys from working-class families who lived out there who probably weren't going to college."

"But you just said there was no war at the time."

"Not then. But a few years later things turned ugly, and draft boards had to submit their quotas of eligible draftees. Fair or not, they usually began with the non-college types—but college guys who'd registered near their schools, like in Westwood or Berkeley where most everyone was a student, found themselves being drafted."

"But not you."

"No. My draft board was one of those that called up the non-college guys first."

"So, someone's in Vietnam right now in your place."

"Yeah, I know. It bothers me, but the opportunity was there, and I figured it would have been stupid to ignore it."

"So, what happened when you graduated?"

I smiled. "Lucky again. After I got my teaching credential, I discovered that just the way my draft board did with college students, they were doing with teachers—giving deferments. Same reason—they had a whole lot of non-professionals to choose from. As far as my draft board is concerned, I can continue my patriotic job of educating young people."

"While thousands of other guys your age— not to mention the Vietnamese—are dying over there."

"Right. While all that death is going on, I get to teach grammar and literature to junior high school kids in Los Angeles."

Mandy patted my knee. "For what it's worth, I think you made the right move."

I nodded in appreciation, and we sat quietly for a moment listening to the end of the album. I think we were both contemplating the unfairness of the draft.

When the turntable clicked off, Mandy asked, "Something to drink?"

"Sure."

She walked into the kitchen and returned with a bottle of Kahlua and a pair of small glasses. She poured each of us a drink, handed me mine, and sat down again.

We toasted each other and sipped.

"What about those lesson plans," I asked her.

"Tomorrow," she whispered, her green eyes staring into mine.

I wanted to kiss her right then. Putting my glass down on the orange crate, I turned off the light and leaned in.

"I hardly know you," she laughed, her face lit up by the bluish glow from the stereo amp that had remained turned on.

"You know me well enough," I said.

Thus, our romance began—which is not to say that we didn't face challenges. I can't speak to the requirements of other jobs, but Mandy and I spent so much of our time outside of school on classroom-prep that we found little chance to do anything else together but schoolwork. Lesson-planning, correcting essays, researching course content—all that extra-curricular stuff made it difficult for us to have time for more traditional dates like going out for dinner or to movies—especially, during the week.

Even so, I had it easier. For Mandy, everything was new. I at least had familiar lessons to rely on. Exploring the art of communication was my favorite. To start all my classes, I'd give the kids a list of rules for grammar and usage—only with a catch. Each rule contained an error that the rule itself addressed: "Don't abbrev" or "Eschew surplusage," for example. When the kids corrected all the errors, they discovered that they'd produced a practical list of ways to improve their writing.

I also liked to highlight how challenging it is to describe what you see. I'd send a student out in the hall, so the kid couldn't observe what I was doing. Once the student was gone, I'd sketch a number of linked circles and squares and triangles on the chalkboard and instruct the class to use their words to recreate my drawing. Then I'd erase my work and bring back in the student who'd been out of the room. Handing over a piece of chalk, I'd tell the kid to draw a design on the board according to the written description a classmate would read aloud.

Most of the time, the new design—a disjointed square here, an elongated circle there—looked nothing like my original. Not only did the lesson make the point—how tough it is to write an accurate description of what's right in front of you—but the goofy drawings that materialized on the board never failed to crack up the class.

As a novice, Mandy had only a handful of models from her student-teaching days to fall back on. One of her most successful lessons centered on an interview assignment which focused on some national issue like the war in Vietnam or the assassination of President Kennedy. She required each kid to read a book about the history of the event and then interview a family member—a mom or dad or aunt or grandparent—who could report their personal involvement with the subject.

One kid reported on his father who in 1960 had served as a delegate for JFK at the Democratic Convention in the L.A. Sports Arena. Another told of an older brother who'd been wounded in Khe Sanh and sent home from Vietnam. Although a parent's involvement sometimes consisted of nothing more than having simply been alive during a happening of note, Mandy reported how a kid's mom or dad would tell her how much they appreciated the status they'd achieved in their children's eyes for having been even distantly related to some significant event in American history

In mid-October, the first meeting-free Tuesday of the semester, Mandy invited me to her apartment for dinner. The evening turned into our first night together.

Agreeing that neither our colleagues nor our boss needed to know how we spent our free time or with whom, we drove to school in separate cars the next morning and managed to arrive at different times.

It was not until I entered the building and saw Jack handing teachers black armbands that I remembered the significance of the date: October 15, 1969. Moratorium Day—a national day of protest. I admit it slipped my mind. Hundreds of thousands of people were gathering across the country to express their rage at America's war in Vietnam—my rage as well—and yet here I was, happy as could be, relishing my time spent with Mandy.

Though some teachers pushed right past Jack, most accepted the armbands and were quick to put them on. As for Vivian Laws, he scowled through the windows in the double-doors of the main office. Yet there was nothing he could do about the display of anti-war sentiment because just a few months earlier the Supreme Court had granted teachers the right to wear political armbands.

"Oh, yeah," I mumbled sheepishly when Jack offered me a black strip of cotton. "I forgot. Thanks."

He raised a tufted eyebrow, but I didn't supply him with any reason to connect the fog I was in with Mandy. "Corny donated the armbands," he said. "She bought them with her own money along with her classroom supplies—no taxpayer funds involved. She has a good heart."

When Mandy caught up to me in the hallway, she too was wearing an armband. "Our students may only be in junior high," she said, "but in a few years the boys will be eligible for the draft."

"Never too early," I agreed, and the two of us marched proudly down the hall together in our matching armbands.

The following evening, Mandy and I returned to The Fox and Hounds to celebrate the one-month anniversary of our first date. As far as I could tell, no one at Phillips had detected our deepening romance, and yet at the end of that same week, Laws and Steele made those upsetting visits to Mandy's classroom. Maybe the timing of those observations had been mere coincidence, but in fact they set off alarm bells in my head.

Chapter Five

Tensions

*A*s disturbing as those back-to-back visits to Mandy's classroom seemed, they paled in comparison with the national news that ripped through the country a few weeks later. While I continued to stress over what Laws and Steele were thinking about Mandy's teaching, horrific accounts of an American slaughter of Vietnamese civilians in the village of My Lai were exploding in the media.

The massacre had occurred in March of the previous year, yet in mid-November of '69, thanks to the dogged reporting of Seymour Hersh, the story was finally coming to light. A troop of American soldiers had murdered hundreds of unarmed Vietnamese villagers, including women and children. Women had been raped, and bodies had been mutilated. Twenty-six American soldiers were charged with the crimes, but only Lt. William Calley, Jr., a platoon leader, would ultimately be convicted.

When news of the slaughter became public, half-a-million marchers gathered in Washington to protest yet again America's continued involvement in the war. It was a story that couldn't be kept out of classrooms, nor should teachers have wanted it to be. With current events a required part of the social studies curriculum, My Lai became a primary topic in all of the department's classes.

Although a "mere" English teacher, I too tried to focus my lessons on the issues of the day. In dealing with literature, however, my topics had to be broader, more thematic. To that end, while the Vietnam War continued, I would assign my ninth-graders poems about war in general by an assortment of poets from Shakespeare to Wilfred Owen to Randall Jarrell. Then I would ask the kids to compose essays about the Vietnam War based on the philosophy expressed in a poem they'd chosen to analyze. What, for example, might their poet have to say about the hostilities in Southeast Asia? About the My Lai Massacre? About protests at home?

In order to help them personalize the distinctions, I would select various students to dramatize the poets they'd written about. (One girl came dressed in army khakis to represent World War I soldier/poet, Siegfried Sassoon.) In a mock press conference, members of the class would ask questions related to Vietnam, and the student-actors would come up with answers based on the texts they'd studied.

In the face of a patriotic question, for example, the student portraying the disillusioned Wilfrid Owen might approximate the poet's celebrated line, "It is neither sweet nor fitting to die for one's country." A humanistic Thomas Hardy could explain how, if not at war, poor Vietnamese and poor Americans would be quick to share a drink. A bitter E.E. cummings might explain how "not-thinking" leads to horrors precisely like My Lai.

In the name of balance, I would present a wide range of views. The mournful pleas of John McCrae to join the military-cause, for instance, contrasted with cummings' philosophy. Hoping to help my students understand the importance of national unity, of the need for people to come together, I always closed the unit with the call to arms delivered by Shakespeare's Henry V at the battle of Agincourt, the speech in which the King calls his fellow soldiers, "We few, we happy few, we band of brothers."

The conflicted reality of American society, of course, worked against the idea of uniting. Individuals took sides; families split apart; political arguments involved life and death. "A teaching deferment?" one of my aunts had scoffed during Thanksgiving dinner that year. "Better to have my boy come home in a box than see him run away with his tail between his legs."

Mandy spent Thanksgiving vacation in New York with her father. I picked her up at LAX on Sunday afternoon at the end of the holiday weekend.

"I missed you," she said, kissing my cheek as soon as she climbed into the Dart.

"I missed you too," I said, offering a quick hug. With school resuming the next day, we had little time for anything else.

"Most of you are probably aware," Vivian Laws said to start Tuesday's faculty meeting, "that the ten-week report cards have just gone out." He laid both his arms on the podium and leaned forward. "I happen to know from reviewing the grade-totals that some of you—" and here he paused to gaze at the unfortunate souls seated directly in front of him—"some of you have once again given too many high marks."

No doubt everyone was thinking of the unhappy fate of the transferred Dr. Falstaff.

"Let me remind you all that we are not in the business of buying affection. Quite frankly, our job is to have people not like us. Education is much more than simply feeding a cult of popularity. Show me a teacher all the youngsters like—" this time his glance swept the entire room— "and I'll show you a poor teacher."

Dead silence.

"Oh," he smirked, "don't think I don't know who you are. Don't think I can't tell whose classes are rowdy until I come to the door. Don't think I can't tell whose students only straighten up when they see me arrive. And don't think for a minute that I don't know which teachers let their students chew gum."

Mandy's jaw tightened at the last two words.

Laws paused again. He understood how to manipulate the silence, how to provide teachers the chance to blanket themselves in guilt.

"Fortunately for all of you," the principal said, still leaning forward, "the Board of Education pays me to be mean." He raised a finger of caution. "Never doubt that it's for your own good. Better to have the criticism come from me than from the outside. Quite frankly, if a parent nails you to the cross, you're going to be nailed hard."

Somebody coughed.

"I want you working all the time," Laws went on. "Believe me when I say: if you step out of line—" here he raised high his right hand, the one missing the little finger, and balled it into a fist— "we're going to come down on you like—" (he slammed his fist down so hard on the podium that some people actually jumped) "—a ton of bricks."

He let the echo reverberate. You could feel the suppression. There was no trace of the sounds that arise in ordinary meetings—no throats clearing, no voices whispering, no chairs scraping. I counted plenty of unhappy faces in the library that day. I watched Randy Stones, the salt-and-pepper haired P.E. coach close his eyes; even Betty Warden, my faithful neighbor, looked down. All in silence.

I knew I had to react. Mandy had found my knee beneath the table and squeezed it hard. I welcomed the connection. But other issues were also prompting me—the administrative visits to Mandy's classroom, the snarky comments about Berkeley, my aunt's insulting comment about avoiding the draft. Then again, maybe I was just tired of listening to Vivian Laws.

In retrospect, however, I believe that it was the Thanksgiving holiday of '69 that prompted a new spirit to rise inside of me. Thanks to the rigid repetition of daily classes, the rhythmic ebb and flow of semesterly calendars, and the predictable accountability of exams and report cards, vacations have a way of providing teachers a psychological pause—a chance to reflect, the opportunity to mark new turning points.

For whatever the reason, during that Thanksgiving break I came to recognize how, by assuming the job of union rep, I had actually staked out the small section of the planet where I had a role. If the Phillips faculty hoped to minimize the exploitation and reduce the victimization we all suffered at the hands of our principal, it fell upon me, the union rep, to get things started.

So I interrupted the meeting. "Mr. Laws," I shouted, waving my arm like a semaphore. I didn't know exactly what I was planning to say, but I realized it was time to step up.

Mandy looked shocked. Throughout the library, heads turned to see who dared disturb the universe.

Laws's eyes narrowed. He was about to speak, but I got to my feet and cut him off. "Before you finish your speech, sir, I want to inform everybody that—" (I hadn't thought out what came next) "—that, that there's going to be a union meeting in my room next week."

"When?" a voice called out.

An excellent question. "I—I'll post the details on the board in the main office."

About the specifics of such a meeting I didn't have a clue. I hadn't called for a union meeting the entire semester. All I knew was that people needed a place to release whatever it was that the silence was stifling. There was lots of murmuring in the library now as if something new may actually have begun incubating in the stillness. When I turned to Mandy, she was smiling at me. As for Laws, he seemed to recognize that he needed to dismiss us.

By the time Mandy and I got to the main office, the details had crystalized in my mind. On the green chalkboard I wrote the time and place of the meeting: next Wednesday, 3:00, my room.

Towards the end of lunch the following day, the cafeteria door swung open, and a stranger marched in. His clothes were conventional enough—a brown tweed jacket, dark slacks, a blue work shirt, and a black bowtie. His round, wire-rimmed glasses gave him an academic look, and yet an incongruous string of orange-and-white love beads circled his neck.

Jack was the first to say his name. "Jeremy Goodman. He used to teach here."

Goodman worked the room on his way to the food counter, shaking hands with some, waving at others. He stopped to flirt with Martha O'Reilly and Annie Smith, the two math teachers who were eating at a table near the door; and he nodded hello to Tiffany Schwartz, the health teacher with the beehive hairdo colored a dull silver. Then he ambled to the counter and after collecting a bowl of minestrone and a plate of spaghetti, paid the kid at the register, noticed our table, and carried his tray over. Awaiting no invitation, he pulled out a chair and sat down next to Mandy.

"I never pass up the chance to meet a pretty face," he deadpanned, raising and lowering his eyebrows Groucho-like while tapping a phantom cigar in the air.

Mandy acknowledged him with a quick, cold smile, and Jack made the introductions. "Jeremy taught English here," he said. "It was his last assignment before going to Vietnam."

In my small world, Jeremy Goodman became the first Vietnam vet I ever met.

The former teacher lifted the white soup bowl and drank from it. Suddenly, he put the bowl down, removed his glasses, and sniffed the air. "Tell you what," he said, screwing up his face, "three years later and this place still smells the same." When he'd finished the soup—he did use a spoon for the vegetables at the bottom—he produced a wrinkled white handkerchief and, removing his glasses, wiped clean the round lenses. Stuffing the cloth in a pocket, he put the glasses back on and turned to the spaghetti.

"You know," he said after sucking up a few strands, "when I worked here, the Old Man never liked me. I used to do stuff like group-counseling. He was afraid I'd fuck up the kids. Plus, I spent too much time talking politics with Union Jack over here." He pointed his fork at the former union rep.

"I remember those days," Jack said.

"I didn't have tenure," Goodman went on, "so Laws let me go. Without a permanent position, I figured, 'What the hell,' and enlisted. Then I was off to war."

"Three years ago?" I said. "I was the only new English teacher hired here three years ago."

"No shit, man?" Goodman put down his fork and gave me a once over. "So, you're my replacement," he said with a chuckle. "Man, if I knew you better, I'd say, 'Congratulations, sucker.' Shit, I might as well say it anyway." He paused to swallow another noodle.

"What are you doing now?" Mandy asked.

"Happy to answer that, doll. It's why I'm here. I'm about to become a sub. After I got back to the States, I tried lots of things: door-to-door selling, social work, even a little stand-up comedy. I wasn't very good."

"Stand-up comedy sounds pretty scary," said Mandy.

Goodman snorted in agreement. "I'll say. It takes lots of nerve—especially with all the drunks and hecklers. But you know what? Man, even with all that shit going down, I've never faced a tougher crowd than a junior high school English class. Bar none."

Goodman speared a few more strands of spaghetti. "But, hey," he said, "none of those jobs agreed with me, so I figured, what the hell, I'll try teaching again. I start subbing next week. And since I still know a few people here, I wanted to get my name on the Phillips sub-list before I go anywhere else."

"You should talk to Annette in the office," Jack said.

"Already have, mate. She's cool with it. Now I'm spreading the word around the faculty."

"Weren't you nervous about running into Mr. Laws?" Mandy asked. "I mean, if he doesn't like you and all."

"Are you serious? After risking my life in Nam? Man, I'm a vet now. You know how that prick likes the army. In fact, when I got here today, he saw me and saluted."

"Impressive," Jack said.

Just then the bell rang, and throughout the room teachers rose to bus their dishes. Goodman took the opportunity to shout out, "Remember! Whenever you need a sub, don't forget to request Jeremy Goodman." A few heads nodded, but nobody said anything. Goodman scanned the room, sniffed again, and scowled.

Later that day, I was reading aloud in Middle English from the Prologue to *The Canterbury Tales* when a student-service-worker brought me a note. Though the kids seemed to hang on every word of the guttural, non-modern sounds of Chaucer's language, the note distracted me. "Mr. Malamud," Annette Avalon had written, "please come to Mr. Laws's office today after school."

As soon as I saw the words, I began to worry. Presumably, I'd done something wrong.

"Did you happen to hear what this is about?" I asked the messenger, a dark-haired girl with braces.

"Nope," she shrugged. "They just told me to deliver the summons."

That was about it—I'd been summoned.

I got through the rest of Chaucer and my last two classes of the day worrying about what had prompted the principal's request. Not long after school ended, I arrived at Laws's door, and after ushering me in, he pointed to an empty chair.

It was my first visit of the year to the principal's office, but during the time I'd been at Phillips, the interior hadn't changed. As usual, the blinds were closed. The only light came from a lamp on Laws's highly-polished desktop. The lamp featured a dark-yellow shade and a tall wood base, which, according to Laws, had been fashioned from a ship's belaying pin. In any case, the lamp provided enough light to illuminate the room and the strange paraphernalia that made up the décor.

I call the interior design a kind of awkward naval chic. On the wall to the left hung three formulaic portraits of antique schooners, their white sails billowing above dark and stormy seas. Next to them was a gleaming wooden ship's wheel the size of a small pizza. To the right hung a strangely mismatched pair of crossed fencing-foils. A thin blade pointed diagonally upward with classic fine-lined grace, but its partner—a makeshift replacement created from a fat Venetian-blind slat painted silver—served only as comic relief.

On the desk, two miniature brass ship's cannons functioned as bookends, supporting a trio of bright-orange binders—local and state education codes, I assumed. Next to the binders stood a delicate model sailing ship complete with faded canvas sails and black, threadlike rigging. In front of the principal himself, a small brass plaque faced outward. As might be expected, it contained a single word: "Captain."

Usually, this particular captain closed the door for meetings with personnel. Today, however, he had left it open. As a result, he had a clear view over my shoulder of the chalkboard on the wall a few yards behind me in the main office.

"The notice you wrote out there," he said, pointing at my announcement, "about a 3:00 meeting next week in your room?"

I turned to look. The lines of sunlight sneaking in between the closed blinds behind Laws's back painted thin horizontal stripes across my writing.

"I'm sure you're aware," Laws said, "that teachers must remain in their classrooms for ten minutes after the end of school. You also know that period six lets out at 2:52, not 2:50. I expect you to change the start-time of your meeting accordingly."

The principal flashed a quick smile and picked up the yellow pencil that was lying in front of him. "You know, Art," he said, aiming the pencil at me as if he were holding a dart, "I've met any number of young teachers who've ruined their careers by pushing too hard. Men and women alike, I should add. I hope you get my meaning."

I took a deep breath. "Understood," I said. Now I could worry about myself as well as Mandy. Technically, he was also right about the timing for the meeting, and I had to do as I was told. Like a resentful kid, I shuffled out to the chalkboard and added the two minutes to the start-time. I couldn't stop myself from grinding the stick of white chalk into the green slate, however, and the chalk snapped in two. Hurling both pieces into a nearby trashcan, I marched out the door as quickly as I could.

Chapter Six

Evaluations I

3:02, Wednesday afternoon. I never expected so many colleagues to show up. Some thirty teachers had squeezed into the student desks in my classroom. Most were union members, but there were a few who were not.

Jack had come, of course. He was standing off to the side, leaning against the wall. Next to him in a front-row seat sat Mandy. I was delighted to have her moral support; and yet as close as the two of us had become, I wanted nothing less than to sign her up as a card-carrying member of our union chapter.

I could understand that she didn't want to be labeled a troublemaker in her first year of teaching —especially after those visits to her classroom from Laws and Steele. But I still had hope. After all, she sympathized with my complaints, and her first-year anxieties hadn't prevented her from wearing a black armband on Moratorium Day.

As luck would have it, Jeremy Goodman also made an appearance. It was his first day of subbing at Phillips. He walked in with Betty Warden a few minutes after most everyone else had gotten there, the jangle of Betty's metallic bracelets heralding their arrival.

I figured that everybody had their own reasons for coming. Some in the crowd may simply have felt disrespected. Others may have feared being transferred, like Mike Falstaff, for crossing Laws. A few more may have dropped by just to see what all the fuss was about. But all things considered, I believed that most people attended because they wanted to vent.

Whatever their motivation, I couldn't fool myself into expecting any sort of success from the meeting. Even I recognized that I was breaking the cardinal rule of organizing: never hold a meeting whose outcome you can't predict. Beyond letting people speak their minds, I had no idea where this might end up.

It wasn't surprising, therefore, that during the first few minutes, nobody volunteered anything. From the nervous expressions on people's faces, I was certain that we all shared the same paranoia. *Big Brother is watching.* Wherever teachers uttered a complaint on the Phillips campus—in their classrooms, in the cafeteria, even in the faculty bathrooms—they worried that their words would get back to Laws. Fear is infectious.

Even though I was standing in the familiar confines of my own classroom surrounded by all my own stuff—my England map, my grammar charts, my author caricatures—I too felt anxious. I myself wondered whether the P.A. speaker mounted on the front wall was also a listening device. Nonetheless, I had to say something.

"Could I have everybody's attention?" I asked.

Immediately, Jack's hand shot up. I had no idea what he was going to say, but I'm sure he sensed the relief I felt when I had someone to call on. All the faces in the room turned in his direction as he stepped forward.

"We all know what's brought us here," he said, running his broad hand across his shiny head. "The way the school is run."

"That's right, Jack," Corny said; and others buzzed agreement.

"We can't be forgetting Dr. Falstaff," Martha O'Reilly said in her Irish accent.

Assorted voices recalled the memory: "Too many A's." "Laws never liked him."

"At least, if you're transferred," observed Tiffany Schwartz, "there's a chance of ending up in a high school. And any high school has to be less of a madhouse than this place."

Murmurs of agreement filled the room.

"The subject matter's more challenging," Tiffany continued. "Older kids just must be easier to reason with. I mean, they're already thinking about colleges and jobs. And, supposedly, administrators have less power. That's what I've heard, anyway. My friends tell me—"

"Thanks, Tiffany," I said, cutting her off. She had a point with which I couldn't disagree. Although

71

I didn't view myself as one of those malcontents who regarded junior highs as nothing more than holding pens for adolescents-run-wild, I could furnish my own hair-raising tales—the girl who wielded a knife in class, the boy who threw desks around the room. But then anyone who knows anything about educators will tell you that teachers are storytellers, people who love anecdotes—especially their own. Given the chance, my colleagues could have gone on recounting "war stories" for the rest of the afternoon.

Martha O'Reilly re-established our goal. "So how do we go about protecting ourselves?" she asked.

"Yeah," Frick agreed. "We all know that Laws does everything by the book. I figure he sleeps with the damned ed code under his pillow."

A dollop of laughter.

Marc Whisk, the art teacher, pushed back the round glasses that had slid down his nose. "You got to give the man credit," he said. "I could never learn all that stuff."

"Marc's got a point," I said. "For all Laws's malaprops and quirks, you have to admit that he knows the rules and regulations."

People nodded, and for an uncomfortable moment silence billowed up again. We were there to complain, yet some of the comments—including my own—bordered on the complimentary. Laws's intricate knowledge of the district rules he used against us seemed the single issue upon which everyone could agree.

Throughout the discussion, Jack had remained standing near the front of the room, obviously waiting for his chance to speak again. When he did, it was to announce a plan. I don't know how long he'd been nursing it since I thought he'd backed away from school politics when he relinquished his union position. But I guess that defying Vivian Laws was too much a part of Jack's nature to give it up completely. Maybe, with his retirement scheduled for the end of the next year, the former rep wanted to fire off a final round.

"Let's evaluate the principal," Jack said. "In fact, let's evaluate all the administrators. In writing. In public. We can create our own evaluation forms like the ones they use on us."

Another momentary hush.

Then Don Frick spoke up. "It wouldn't be official. It wouldn't have any teeth. What's the big deal about telling Laws what we think of him? For starters, he probably already knows."

"And doesn't give a shit," Jeremy Goodman added.

Penelope Martinez brushed at the blue chalk dust on her nose. "Hasn't he already told us," she asked in her quiet voice, "that being disliked by teachers is indicative of being a good principal?"

Lots of people nodded. I couldn't remember Penelope ever speaking at a meeting before.

"Worse," Betty chimed in, "he's told us that he believes the same applies to teachers—good ones shouldn't be liked by their students. You know, down with cults of personality."

More nods.

"The point is," Jack said, "not only do we give our evaluations to Laws and the others, but we make copies and send them to our PTA. Let the parents know how we feel."

A few murmurs of approval hummed through the group.

"To make things even more interesting," Jack said, "we can give copies to our local superintendent. Heck, we can send copies to members of the school board like Dr. Torres—he always claims he's on our side. He might even enjoy hearing what we think."

Jack was upping the stakes. Such a plan required a whole lot of nerve, and I wasn't sure how many people would be willing to go along. It was a daring proposal; I had to give him that. So daring, in fact, that he hadn't even shared it with me. Maybe he worried that I wouldn't approve.

The truth is, I liked the idea. It was responsible, reasonable, and respectful. After all, the forms would even allow you to compliment the principal—if you wanted to.

"Do we have to sign them?" Frick asked.

"I don't know," Jack said, rubbing his head again. "I guess they could be anonymous."

Frick laughed. "You know Laws—he'll figure out who we are from our handwriting. You'll see. He'll get back at all of us."

"It sounds to me like washing our dirty clothes in public," Tiffany Schwartz said.

I exchanged glances with Jack. Maybe evaluating Laws wasn't such a good idea after all. For the plan to work, we were going to have to do a lot of persuading.

Then Jeremy Goodman stood up, his glasses flashing. "I haven't been here in a long time," he said, "and right now I'm only a sub, so maybe I don't have much of a right to say anything." He looked at me for permission.

"Go ahead," I told him. "You know this place better than most. Speak your mind."

"Well," he said, "no offense, but in the past three years this faculty hasn't changed a whole lot. Sure, some of the faces are different, but I can still smell the fear. It's like the stink in the cafeteria."

"That's right," said Betty, raising a fist. Her bracelets jingled in accompaniment.

"You think you're riled up about what happened to Falstaff?" Goodman asked. "Shit, nobody's going to do a fucking thing."

Suddenly, Tiffany Schwartz sprang up, her fluffed silver hair adding a couple of inches to her height. "I don't have to sit here and listen to his foul language," she proclaimed and stalked out of the room.

"Sorry about that," Goodman said, as the clack of Tiffany's heels faded away in the hall. "Free speech is part of my nature. Steinbeck said something about taking away the working man's profanity and you're left with a silent man." He put his hands in his back pockets and turned towards Betty. "Now where was I?"

"You just said," she whispered loud enough for everyone to hear, "'nobody's going to do a fucking thing.'"

Goodman grinned at her. "Listen," he said, "in the army we had schmucks like Laws commanding us. Administrators, officers—they're all cut from the same cloth—people who think the world belongs to them, people who think they understand what's good for everyone else."

"That's Laws," I heard someone mutter.

Goodman grinned again. "Back in Nam, I remember officers marching around dead drunk in their underwear, pistols strapped to their sides. They were so out of it they couldn't tell what was going on. They ordered a firefight one night—tracers and bombs and shit lit up the sky. In the morning, all we found was a dead cow."

"Point?" somebody asked.

"Those officers thought they knew what was up, but they didn't know squat. If you want to protect yourselves from leaders like that, look out for number one." He held up his index finger to dramatize the argument.

People stared blankly.

Goodman looked around the room. "Don't you get it?" he asked no one in particular. "If each of you protects yourself from the big shots who think they know what's best for you, then by extension you're all automatically working together to protect the entire group."

Goodman sat down, and a few people in the audience nodded as if they finally understood. Mandy's eyebrows arched quizzically while I wondered how I could use any of this to organize the union chapter. Whatever people thought about Jeremy Goodman, it still seemed that they were reluctant to accept Jack's challenge.

Jack himself came to the rescue. "We'll start slowly," he said, begging the question of whether we should be evaluating anybody in the first place. "I'll wait until Christmas to draw up the forms. That way, we can meet after the break to see if we still want to proceed."

"What do you say?" I asked the group. "We'll have plenty of time when we come back from vacation to vote on whether or not we should be moving forward."

Amid exchanged whispers and bobbing heads, I was surprised to discern a sense of agreement floating around the room. But why not? People wouldn't be committing themselves to anything real just yet, and there was winter break to provide time for reconsidering the entire conspiratorial enterprise. After the holidays, everyone would still get the chance to reject the idea if that was what they wanted.

I believe it was the cautionary nature of the plan that ultimately swayed people. When I asked for a show of support, the majority of teachers in the room—many reluctantly, a small few with actual enthusiasm—raised their hands. Mandy did not. Nonetheless, in those final moments of the meeting, however tentatively, the movement to evaluate the administrative staff had begun.

Chapter Seven

Winter Break

*I*n December of 1969, comedian Bob Hope
and singer Connie Stevens braved the dangers of war
to spread the Christmas spirit among the American
troops in Vietnam. At Phillips Junior High, it was
the distribution of the fall-semester teacher-reviews
that marked the start of the holiday season.
Contracts, salary increases, tenure—all are
determined by satisfactory evaluations, and Vivian
Laws seemed to take special pleasure in handing out
his judgments just before the two-week winter break.

"It's my way of increasing the good cheer,"
he said when teachers complained about getting their
assessments a day or so before the holiday. To a
certain extent, he was right—some people did feel
good, but only those very few who got
complimentary reports. Most teachers, especially
the ones without tenure, went home for the break
destined to spend their two-week vacation
ruminating over the criticisms.

In the case of tenured teachers, only if they
mess up so badly that they offer their heads on a
platter do they need to worry about the principal's

evaluations. Though such a teacher might get verbally criticized or receive a negative review or even, like Mike Falstaff, be forcibly transferred at the whim of the principal—they hardly ever get fired. As a case in point, in order to rid himself of a tenured music teacher who'd somehow crossed him but whom Laws couldn't sack, the principal simply shut down the music department. No music classes for the kids, no job for the teacher. He had to transfer to another school.

As a tenured teacher, I wasn't particularly surprised when Laws handed me a strong evaluation. I thanked him for his support; but as I was about to leave his office, he couldn't resist a parting shot.

"Remember," he said, "it's not what a principal puts on paper that matters; it's what he tells other administrators at meetings or on the phone." To emphasize his point, he held his right fist to his ear as if he were on the telephone—thumb up, little finger out, except, of course, there was no little finger.

"I'm looking forward to a positive evaluation," Mandy said as the day of her reckoning approached. "No one's come back to watch me teach since those two visits in November, so they'll be relying on what Sam has to say. Right?"

"Sure," I said, hoping she was correct. After all, she'd shown me the many lesson-plans her department chair, Sam Turner, had labeled "Great!" in red marker. In fact, he'd told Mandy he had such confidence in her work that she didn't need to submit her plans to him anymore.

On the other hand, although I didn't say it out loud, there was always the possibility that Laws would pay no mind to anything Sam had to say, which is why I wasn't totally surprised when Mandy marched angrily into my classroom at the start of lunch on the Friday before Christmas break.

"Laws doesn't like my lesson planning," she fumed, throwing the evaluation down on my desk. "He says my lessons need more structure. He says I should—" (she jabbed a finger at the offending sentence on the paper as she read it aloud) "— 'try teaching more creatively instead of relying on basics.'"

"Mandy," I said, glancing down at the form, "this is Vivian Laws you're talking about. If you taught more creatively, he'd tell you to teach more basics."

"What do you mean *'if'*? When a teacher brings her own drawings to class, that's about as creative as you can get."

I tapped the evaluation grid at the bottom of the page. "Look here. This is the important part." Laws had checked 'Meets or Exceeds Standard Performance' in every box. "You can't do any better. Forget his comments; this puts you on the fast track to tenure."

Still breathing heavily, Mandy looked down and examined the checked boxes. "There's not a word," she sneered, "nothing, about what Sam Turner has said."

"Consider the source, Mandy. Laws never says anything nice about anybody. Especially when they're new. It's part of the intimidation process. You got the 'meets or exceeds.' That's all that matters."

She crossed her arms. "Easy for you to say. You've got tenure."

I couldn't argue with her logic, so I changed the subject. "Let's go to lunch."

"Okay," she said sharply. "But I resent his timing. It's a lousy Christmas present."

Before a long vacation, it's tough to get much teaching done. Daydreams about the upcoming break make concentrating difficult for students and teachers alike. Even as I stood in front of my classes, I was envisioning the two weeks away from school that Mandy and I were about to share. Nonetheless, in the final hours of the final day before winter break, I was determined to offer my students a lesson that contained some educational value.

"Spelling-Baseball" was my plan, a game dependent upon the accurate spelling of the vocabulary words my kids have studied in class. To create two teams, you divide the class in half. As the players' "at-bats" come around, they get to choose from "single" to "home run," depending on the difficulty-level of the word that the kid hopes to spell. Get it right, and get on the appropriate base; spell it wrong and be called out—a simple premise. The secret lies in organizing the words in advance according to their difficulty.

I'd drawn a rough baseball diamond on the chalkboard to keep track of the baserunners and the number of runs. In the middle of the fourth inning, the score was tied 5-5, and the team at bat had the bases loaded.

"I want a home run," announced the boy whose turn it was. He was hoping for a grand slam.

I checked my list of most-difficult words. "Spell 'epiphany,'" I said.

With the game on the line, both sides of the room trained their eyes on the "batter."

"E—" he began, "P—"

Suddenly, the door burst open, and into the room danced a properly rotund, white-bearded, red-suited Santa Claus. "Ho, ho, ho," Santa chortled as he threw his arms around me.

The class exploded in laughter, Spelling-Baseball immediately forgotten.

"Do you know what little Artie Malamud always wanted for Christmas?" Santa prodded the class.

"No!" the kids shouted in unison.

"Grammar books," came the answer.

A collective groan filled the room. Somebody in the back yelled, "Dud."

Now Santa was passing out glistening red suckers wrapped in crinkly cellophane.

I laughed along with everybody else. But Santa was already waving good-bye and preparing to visit the next classroom on his list. I knew Spelling-Baseball was a lost cause; there was no way I was going to recover the attention of the kids.

It was another seasonal tradition, and everyone recognized that Santa was Vivian Laws. Judging from the fun the principal seemed to have each year he donned the red suit, I presumed he was reviving some vestige of the interest in teaching that must have attracted him to the profession way back when.

The distribution of faculty rosters also marked the holiday at Phillips. During the week before the break, Annette Avalon typed the lists in red ink on light-green paper and sealed them in manila envelopes stamped "Confidential." Before placing them in our mailboxes, she kept them neatly stacked underneath an eight-inch desk gnome outfitted in a dark-brown tunic and matching pointed hat.

Each roster contained the names and addresses of the entire staff, making it easy for the people who actually did such things to send out greeting cards, party invitations, and even—should anyone feel so motivated—holiday presents. At the

84

very least, each member of the faculty could count on receiving a seasonal card from Vivian Laws. His 1969 entry featured a kneeling George Washington at Valley Forge, the Christmas star shining appropriately bright in the dark sky high above George's bewigged head.

Among the other season's greetings that arrived in the mail was the invitation to the annual Phillips Christmas party. For the fourth year in a row, Abe Norovsky and his wife had agreed to host; and thanks to Annette Avalon's rosters, they had sent out invitations to the entire faculty.

Mine lay on the yellow Formica table in my breakfast nook where Mandy and I were drinking coffee.

"No way I'm socializing with the principal," she said. "Not after that disgusting review."

I leaned across the table and took her hand. "Come on. He checked off all the right boxes, and a Christmas party would be the perfect time to show everybody we're a couple."

"As if most people don't already know. And what about Laws? Do you really think we have to let him in on our private lives?"

"What does it matter? We can go public on our own terms—in front of Laws and everybody else."

Mandy remained silent, as if she were thinking it over. "Well," she drawled, "as long as I can spend the rest of the break just with you, I guess it'll be okay."

"A cemetery with lights"—that's what we used to call the San Fernando Valley in high school. There were more lights these days, especially in the evenings at Christmas time, and they were beginning to turn on as we exited the San Diego Freeway and drove west on Ventura. The Norovskys lived in a two-story house that occupied much of a low-lying hill just south of "The Boulevard." Like the rest of the neighborhood, the place featured a broad lawn, rounded arches, and a roof of terracotta-tile.

"Southern-California Spanish," Mandy said. "Kind of like my place, only a lot larger."

Thanks to all the cars lining the street, we had to park two blocks away. Even so, you could hear the thumping beat of Eric Burden and the Animals wailing about "The House of the Rising Sun." I carried our gift, a bottle of red wine, as Mandy and I made our way along the edge of the street—there were no sidewalks—towards the flagstone path that led to the Norovskys' front door. From a holly wreath hung a piece of paper with the word "Enter." Mandy's fingers found mine, and hand-in-hand we walked in.

Bright lights and cigarette smoke struck us as soon as we entered, and the music continued thumping away. Yet it was the Norovskys' huge Christmas tree that dominated the living room. The tree was so tall that the tip had been bent in order to squeeze the white angel in sideways at the ceiling. Red, green, and blue fairy lights spiraled around the branches, and among the needles dangled countless ornaments—most of them mementos of the Norovskys' travels: a gold-plated miniature of Hearst Castle; a white, plastic model of the Hotel Del; a group of tiny baseball players from the Hall of Fame in Cooperstown. Adding to the dazzle, a tabletop of glass globes, each full of tiny snowflakes, refracted the colors of the winking bulbs on the tree.

At the far end of the room, I could make out Betty Warden in a pink, tie-dyed dress, whispering into the ear of Jeremy Goodman as they slow-danced together in spite of the fast beat of the music. Tonight, Jeremy wore jeans and a sweater, but the orange-and-white beads still circled his neck.

Coronas in hand, Randy Stones, Don Frick, and Abe Norovsky were sharing stories, and we joined them just in time to hear Stones proclaim, "Everybody knows the old man likes to dress up like Santa Claus. But he always ignores the P.E. classes. Too far to go, I guess." Stones pushed back his grizzled hair and took a pull on the bottle. "Well, on Friday he rode out to the basketball courts on a mini-sweeper—one of those things they drive around to clean up after lunch."

"Like a sleigh, right?" Norovsky shouted to be heard above the music.

Stones nodded. "You should have seen him. The kids were playing basketball, and out he comes like Santa. As soon as he got close—what do you think? They all ran off the court and mobbed the guy."

"Well, sure," Mandy said. "What else would you expect?" It was more of a statement than a question.

"Right on!" Stones cried, waving the Corona.

I scanned the room. I wanted to be sure that the principal himself wasn't lurking nearby, especially if Mandy got overly critical. Then again, unless Stones was too drunk to care, I figured that the P.E. teacher wouldn't be complaining so loudly if he knew that Laws was in the vicinity.

"But here's the thing," Stones went on. "The old man wasn't expecting the kids to get so hyped, and he got pissed off. In fact, he got so pissed off that he ordered our whole department to meet with him after school—right before vacation. The whole department."

"Asshole," Frick said.

"What could he possibly have to tell you?" I asked.

"He lectured us on the importance of keeping kids in class. 'What if there was an emergency?'"

"Like an airplane crash," Frick said.

"Great way to start a vacation," Stones muttered.

Norovsky just shook his head. Administrator that he was, he wasn't about to badmouth the boss.

"Let's get something to drink," Mandy said to me.

I was still hanging on to the bottle of wine we'd brought and was only too happy to find a place to put it.

Mandy steered me under a high archway into the dining room. Though full of people, it was a little quieter in there, and a long table offered up all sorts of goodies. There were red plastic bowls brimming with chips and guacamole; a large, green platter filled with yellow cheese slices and pink cold cuts fanned out like a half-circle of playing cards; and a long wicker basket loaded with dark and light baguettes.

At the far end of the table, just beyond a shimmering bowl of red punch, stood a battalion of red and white wine bottles. I placed our red next to the others, picked up a pair of clear-plastic glasses, and from an open bottle of Chianti poured generous amounts for Mandy and me.

Tiffany Schwartz sidled up next to us and poured her own. With the music still loud enough to make talking difficult, the three of us held up our glasses and motioned a silent toast before sampling our drinks.

A moment later Abe Norovsky, a cigarette poking out from the middle of his goatee, emerged from the living room and inched his way through the maze of people congregating around the food. Holding paper plates piled high with cheese and salami and commandeering glasses full of wine, the crowd formed quite the gauntlet; but Abe, grooving to the music all the while, made his way into the kitchen. Seconds later, he returned with a Corona in each hand.

"Great party," Mandy shouted at him.

He nodded in acknowledgment as he bobbed by and disappeared somewhere back in the living room. The Rolling Stones' "Satisfaction" was now blasting, and despite all the haze, I could see Betty and Jeremy still locked in the same slow dance they'd been in when we'd arrived. Funny how I'd worried about revealing Mandy's and my new relationship, and here were Betty and Jeremy presenting themselves as a couple to anyone who cared to look.

Just then, through the archway to the dining room strode a tall, middle-aged blonde. She wore a bright floral print of blues and yellows accented with a white silk scarf. I recognized her from previous parties, and I gave a quick eye-shift at Mandy so she wouldn't miss the newcomer.

"Who—?" she mouthed, but then she saw Vivian Laws trailing behind and realized that the woman was the principal's wife.

We watched as Laws poured two glasses of white wine and collected some chips and guacamole on a paper plate. He handed one glass to his wife and balanced the other on his plate as they moved away from the table.

"Be careful, Viv," his wife said. "You're going to spill."

"It's all right, "the principal protested.

"I know you, Viv. It's going to spill."

Suddenly, Laws realized that people were watching. "I tell you, it's all right," he said a little too loudly and jerked away from her, upsetting the glass. White wine splashed onto the gray carpet.

"U.S.P.," a voice over my shoulder whispered just loud enough for me to hear. I turned to see Don Frick nodding knowingly in Laws's direction. "Unresolved sexual problems, good buddy," he translated.

Betty Warden, who by now had let go of Jeremy long enough to get something to eat, arrived at the table just in time to observe the spreading stain on the rug at Laws's feet.

"Better lay off the hard stuff, Mr. Laws," she joked.

Norovsky came to the rescue, grabbing some paper napkins to mop up the spill. At the same time, Laws's wife hustled the principal off to some other room.

"At least, it was white wine," said Tiffany Schwartz, patting the silver bubble that was her hair. "It's easier to clean."

Though the rumble of the bass reverberated throughout the house, the den, to which Mandy and I now worked our way, was quieter than the dining room. Dressed in his usual dark suit and tie, Jack was sitting on a brown leather couch talking to Penelope Martinez. Bald Marlon Piff —the kids called him "Chrome Dome"—and gray-haired Brigitte Summerfield had commandeered two of the many folding chairs set up around the room. There was no sign of Laws.

Standing off by herself and nursing a glass of Chianti stood the blond and stately English teacher Sarah Mertz. She'd grown up somewhere in the South, and at our English department meetings we never tired of listening to her discuss poetry. She'd keep our attention with her slow, mellifluous pronunciation. We loved the way she said, "on-o-mat-o-*poe*-ia." She'd purse her lips at the start of the fifth syllable and then coat the final diphthongs with a measured, honey-like lilt.

Mandy waved at Jack and Penelope. "Where's Jack's wife," Mandy asked. "I wanted to meet her."

"Myrna," I said. "He always comes to these affairs by himself. He says that Myrna prefers staying home rather than attending parties where a bunch of teachers sit around and talk shop."

"No shop talk for us," Mandy said, putting her arm around my waist and pointing me in the direction of the curving central staircase. "Let's explore the house."

We climbed the stairs, but couldn't avoid the music; Norovsky's stereo piped the sound upstairs as well. The Beatles were singing about "all the lonely people" when we discovered the solitary Jeremy Goodman planted cross-legged on the floor of a darkened, sweet-scented bedroom. In the narrow rectangle of hall-light shining through the half-open doorway, he sat smoking what looked like a green cigar.

"Want some?" he rasped, thrusting the thing in our direction. "Thai stick from Nam. It's good shit, man."

Smoking anything never appealed to me, not even back in Berkeley where stuff was easy to find. But here in the late '60s with our boss around, I was too cautious to even think about doing anything like that.

Mandy hooked my arm and led me back through the hall and down the stairs.

In the dining room, empty plates and drained bottles had joined the food still remaining on the table, and the aroma of perking coffee filled the air. With Laws and his wife nowhere to be seen— presumably they'd left—Mandy and I succumbed to the allure of the blinking Christmas tree and made our way back to the living room. Mercifully, somebody had turned down the music, and the two of us took advantage of some available space on the couch next to Betty.

A few moments later, Corny Whittaker staggered in. Though she was holding only a napkin, her husband, a ruddy-faced fellow with thinning gray hair, followed, her vodka in hand. The glass was only half-full, but had Corny been carrying it, there was no way the drink wouldn't have spilled. As it was, she made it to a nearby folding chair and managed to collapse onto the seat.

"Corny's quite the drinker, you know," Betty said to me. "Jack couldn't deal."

Mandy leaned in to hear the conversation. "Jack?" she asked

I didn't get the reference either.

"Oh, you didn't know? They used to be a couple. Years ago. Before Jack met Myrna. Corny tries to do the right thing, but stress brings it out. I'm sure Jack's plan to evaluate the principal hasn't helped."

"Her husband doesn't seem to help either," said Mandy.

"Hugh? Not hardly. He doesn't take her problem seriously."

Although Corny sat safely ensconced in her chair, her maneuverings had caused her to drop the napkin she'd been holding. Leaning to her left to retrieve it, she stretched too far and actually toppled out of the chair.

There were gasps of concern, explosions of laughter, and cries of "Are you all right?" "Everything okay?" Randy Stones helped Hugh get Corny back into her chair.

Suddenly, Jack appeared. It took him only a moment to understand the situation. "For God's sake, Hugh," he said, "she's out of control. Take her home!"

There was a pleading in Jack's voice that I'd never heard before. Hugh laughed and motioned for him to calm down. At first, Jack looked as if he were going to reply. Then he simply turned and stalked angrily out of the house.

Corny, having taken the drink from her husband, now stood up and leaning against his shoulder, allowed him to guide her out of the room.

I knew it was almost Christmas and that we were supposed to be full of holiday cheer. Yet despite all the partying, I felt sad.

Mandy and I spent virtually all of winter break together in my apartment. Set off in the back as my place was, there was little noise and plenty of privacy. Not only did the solicitors who invaded the larger building in front not notice me, but also, thanks to the outside metal stairs leading up to my door, you could usually hear anybody who might be approaching. Even the bad guys ignored me. On one occasion, the apartments in the front building were robbed; mine was left alone.

The seclusion didn't keep my landlady, Mrs. Gross, away, however. She was always shuffling by to dump her trash in the bins below my windows; and whenever she saw me, she would shoot disapproving looks my way. I could tell that she didn't like the idea of Mandy's staying with me during the vacation.

I, on the other hand, never wanted those two weeks to end.

Ever practical, Mandy offered an alternative point of view. "I love our time together, Art," she said, "but at the risk of downplaying my personal charm, just maybe you want this vacation to keep on going so you can put off dealing with the evaluations Jack's been working on."

Union rep or not, I didn't want to argue the point. In fact, I can assure anyone who cares that Jack's proposal was not the source of my reluctance to return to school. During the winter break of 1969, evaluating the administrators at Phillips had absolutely no effect on my plans. I simply wanted to spend as much time as possible with Mandy.

Chapter Eight

Evaluations II

*J*ack held the paper high. "Notice how I've divided these forms."

He was speaking to many more teachers that afternoon than the number who'd come to the meeting in my classroom before the break. On this occasion, all forty seats were filled, and a handful of people were standing in the back.

"You'll have the chance to evaluate each administrator in one of three columns," Jack explained. "You can mark *excellent, satisfactory* or *unsatisfactory* based on how effective you think their skills are—you know, leadership, rapport, responsiveness."

"Very cool," observed Betty Warden.

"Look over the pages," Jack said. "Make sure you have four, one for each administrator."

People began scanning the printed sheets Jack had handed them when they'd entered the room. You had to give him credit; he'd prepared well during winter break. While Mandy and I had been preoccupied with each other, he'd been writing, photocopying, and assembling his evaluation forms.

He'd even used black ink, a nice touch that provided a professional look in comparison with the dull purple of most school copy-machines.

Mandy was sitting on the aisle at one side of the room; and I stood next to her, reading the forms over her shoulder. In reality, Jack had shown them to me before the meeting, so I could afford to be distracted. Today Mandy had braided her hair into a single red plait, and sparkles of light danced among the intricacies of the weave whenever she tilted her head.

But I digress.

Corny Whittaker broke the silence. "I don't think you should distribute these things without letting Mr. Laws see them first."

Everyone looked up. Corny was sitting in the rear of the room, and people up front turned to get a better view. Don Frick began clicking his pen.

I'm sure everyone there had a different opinion about what had prompted Corny's concern. Personally, I thought that letting Laws get first crack at the evaluations was Corny's polite way of preventing an unpleasant confrontation later on. She taught homemaking, after all, and that included good manners.

Then again, from what Betty had told us at the Christmas party, for all I knew, Corny might have thought she was protecting Jack. A few people must have worried that Corny was having second thoughts, and others might even have believed that something sinister was going on. Maybe Laws had gotten wind of our meeting and stationed a spy among us.

Clever, if true. Yet of all the people on the faculty who might be fronting for the principal, Corny Whittaker was the last person I'd suspect. (Somebody like Nelly Knopf, the kiss-up science teacher, would've made a more likely candidate. Everybody knew Nelly wanted to become an administrator, but she wasn't even at our meeting.) As for Corny, she would never turn against her colleagues, especially not against Jack. Sure, she had her demons—we'd all seen her after too many drinks at Norovsky's party—but based on her sense of decency, I could never picture her betraying her friends. It simply wasn't a nice thing to do.

"Why should Laws get to see the things before we hand them out?" I asked her.

"Whose side are you on, Corny?" somebody standing behind her had the temerity to demand.

She turned in her chair to answer. "I'm not here to spy for Mr. Laws if that's what you're thinking. I just don't believe it's right for us to sneak around and give out these forms without letting him see them first. It's not fair."

Don Frick put down the pen he was clicking. "Since when has he been fair to us?"

Murmurs of encouragement confirmed the sentiment.

"Fairness," I said to myself, "the rope with which we hang ourselves."

"Corny," said Jack, "you and I have worked together for quite a while now. We've watched a lot of administrators come and go. You know as well as I do that if Laws sees these forms first, he'll never let us hand them out."

Corny stood up. "I just think we shouldn't be accused of going behind his back. That's all. It creates too much ill will." She paused for a moment, fidgeting with the hem of her pink blouse.

"What do you propose?" I asked.

"I'll tell you what," Corny said, standing a bit straighter. "If and when we actually vote to use them, I'll distribute the forms to everyone myself—as long as you agree to let me show them to Mr. Laws beforehand."

Jack looked at me for direction. Mandy caught his gaze and peered at me as well.

To be honest, I hadn't given the distribution of the forms much thought. I guess I figured that if we approved them, I would be the one to give them out. I certainly wouldn't place them in the teachers' mailboxes—too easy for Laws or his flunkies to remove them. I thought I might traverse the campus during my free period and personally deliver the forms to each teacher. But I saw no problem in handing the job off to Corny. As long as she promised she'd actually distribute them, I fully expected she'd come through. I nodded quickly at Jack, feeling like we'd just selected the mouse to bell the cat.

That was it then. We took the vote to evaluate the administration, and to my great surprise, everyone there supported the idea. Even Mandy. I suppose the dissidents hadn't bothered to show up.

"I'll go see Mr. Laws tomorrow at lunch," Corny volunteered. "I'll tell him what we're going to do, and then I'll hand out the forms. It's only fair," she repeated.

With our strategy decided, I adjourned the meeting, and Mandy and I headed for the parking lot.

Jack caught up to us on the walkway. "Having Corny circulate the forms isn't a bad strategy. Coming from her instead of the union leadership, we'll appear more grassroots."

Mandy agreed. "I just hope she doesn't get herself into some kind of trouble over this."

I was thinking the same thing.

"It was a mistake to send her in alone," Jack grumbled the next day. There were just a few minutes remaining in the lunch period, and Corny had been in Laws's office for most of the half-hour. To blur any connection between her mission and the union, Jack and I had positioned ourselves in a stairwell far down the empty hall but still close enough to peer out of our hideaway to see the main-office door.

The longer it remained shut, the more I believed Jack was right. Without witnesses, Laws could do his intimidating any way he wanted. That was part of his method. Even if your classroom was empty following one of his visits, he'd require you to show up in his office, his home turf, so he could lecture you with the door closed.

Jack and I continued to wait. Something was bound to happen. Lunch was almost over, and soon kids would be flooding the halls.

At last, the office door opened, and Corny entered the hallway. She took a moment and leaned against the wall to steady herself. Clearly, whatever Laws had told her in there had shaken her up. Jack and I hurried to her side, but she shrugged us off.

"I don't want to talk about it," she said. "Just forget what I told everybody yesterday. I'm not going to distribute the forms."

"Are you okay?" Jack demanded.

Corny wiped a hand across her brow. "He threatened to sue me if I gave them out—for defamation of character. I don't know about you, but a lawsuit is not something I want to deal with. If you're smart, you'll wait until after the special meeting tomorrow morning before you do anything silly." With that, she managed to turn and walk unevenly down the corridor in the direction of the bathroom.

Jack and I looked at each other.

"Damn!" he exploded. "How does any teaching get done around here the way that man treats people?"

"What special meeting?" I wanted to know.

As if in answer to my question, the passing bell rang; and almost immediately we were submerged in a torrent of kids streaming in from the lunch court.

Jack stood his ground, staring into the ever-more-crowded hallway. It was as if he could still see Corny walking away. "I'm guessing he threatened her with more than defamation of character."

"How so?"

"Who knows? He can make anything up." Somehow able to ignore the hundreds of kids swirling around us, Jack said, "Corny's heart is in the right place, but I don't think she's got the strength to stand up to the guy. And just yesterday she was trying to be fair to him."

I nodded. "And there were some people at the meeting dumb enough to think she might have been one of his spies."

"Not hardly," he said, still managing to block out the kids. "As long as I've known her, she's always supported justice and fairness. No, what gets me is that those are my forms. I should have been the one in that office taking the heat, not her."

Slowly, the traffic in the hallway began to thin, a reminder that it was time for us to get to class.

"I think Corny's right," I said. "We should hold off giving out the forms until after whatever this meeting is tomorrow. We need to hear what Laws has to say. If he really is out to screw us, we ought to know it in advance."

"We've got to protect Corny," Jack insisted. "We got her into this mess. It's not right." Having said his piece, he marched off through the streams of kids with the same sense of outrage he'd revealed when he'd stormed out of Norovsky's house at the faculty Christmas party.

Two hours after Vivian Laws's lunchtime session with Corny, the principal announced on the P.A. a special pre-school meeting scheduled to take place the next morning in the faculty cafeteria. It would deal with what he vaguely termed "union activities."

To arrive together at the meeting, Jack and I met early the next day in the main office. It was so chilly a January morning that as we hurried through the quad, we could see our breath in the cold. The two of us were the first teachers to arrive though the custodial crew had set up the cafe well before we ever got there.

All the circular tables had been pushed back against the walls. In their place, a group of rectangular tables had been arranged to form a squared-off U. It was obvious that Laws was going to sit at the head—the bottom of the "U"—near the door. The rest of us would fill in the sides.

"So much for equal seating," I said.

"So much for any debate," Jack replied.

We selected a pair of seats about ten feet cater-cornered from where we figured the principal would hold court. As we were settling in, a blast of cold air signaled the arrival of Betty Warden. Wrapped in a dark-green parka with fake-fur lining, she struggled through the doorway, doing her best to balance book bag, briefcase, and cup of coffee.

Within the next few minutes, thirty others, all bundled in warm coats and heavy jackets, filed in.

"Hey there, good buddy," Frick greeted me, "I hear this is where the action is." He gave me a thumbs-up before taking a seat.

At precisely 7:30, Vivian Laws entered the cafeteria. Dressed in a light-gray trench coat, the principal was all business. He talked to no one, smiled at no one, looked at no one. Like an eager valet, Roland Swett hustled in after him, trying to match his boss' quick steps. Once they were both seated, the principal produced his yellow legal pad. Between the lapels of his long gray coat, you could see the wide apron of a navy-blue tie.

Laws began by clearing his throat. Then he leaned forward, his bulk teetering at the front end of his chair, his knees slowly opening and closing beneath the tabletop. "Since this is such an important meeting," he announced, raising the yellow pad, "I've brought along written comments. I want to read them to you, so there will be no misunderstanding on your part as to my meaning."

The principal smoothed down the pages in front of him while nervous teachers exchanged worrisome glances. "'It has come to my attention,'" he read, "'that a small group of people on this faculty desire to write evaluations of this administration. Now the concept of observing educators at work is a time-honored practice. But the Education Code clearly states . . .'"

He went on reciting the dull, bureaucratic business as if he were reading a long-winded entry from an encyclopedia. Only the occasional clatter of dishes or whoops of laughter from the cooks in the kitchen interrupted him.

When he finally got to claiming interest in our plan, however, people took note. "'Many of you,'" he read on, "'may be surprised to learn that in the spirit of educational progress, I welcome such an evaluation.'"

Skeptical glances bounced around the room.

"'I speak for Mr. Swett here, as well as for the other administrators, when I say that all of us feel we can only profit from receiving constructive criticism.'"

Swett nodded in agreement although the furrows in his brow suggested otherwise.

"'However,'" Laws read, "'it has also come to my attention that some malcontents on this faculty are simply not satisfied with constructive comments. All they want to do is tear down the structure we've built over the years.'" Here he looked up and spoke off-the cuff. "Oh, I know that some of you think I'm autocratic, and with that I must agree. But it's in the interest of having kids of all colors gathering here together like healthy, red-blooded Americans, and I'm here to tell you that I'll do everything in my power to make that happen."

"Whatever that means," I said to myself.

"But be forewarned," he announced, returning to his text. "'I have no intention of letting some misguided teachers attack me or my staff under the cover of anonymous questionnaires. I am not going to allow a handful of troublemakers destroy what I have created here at Phillips.'" At this point, he slowed his cadence, which made his speech sound all the more accusatory. "'You have drawn up these so-called evaluations on school-district paper. Under the advisement of the lawyers at district headquarters, I hereby order you to destroy them all by ten o'clock this morning.'"

Silence greeted the command, and Laws slowly scanned the room. I couldn't decide which was worse, the imperious tone of his message or our earlier expectations of hopefulness that were now escaping from the faculty cafe like air from a popped balloon.

Jack's gravelly voice interrupted the quiet. "With due respect, Mr. Laws," he said, eyes flashing, "I paid for Xeroxing those forms myself—on my own store-bought paper, and you have no right to tell anyone to destroy them. They're not school district property; they're mine."

"Ooooh!" I could imagine kids saying. "Moded! Shot down!" And just like that, our momentum began regaining traction.

Practicality forced Laws to break away from his script. "Well," he said, his face reddening, his legs moving faster. "Well, well, well."

The principal sat silenced for a moment; and when he resumed, his voice no longer possessed the robotic quality it had taken on when he'd been reading aloud. "I most certainly do have the right," he said in a firm but singsong voice, "to inform you that it is illegal to evaluate administrators and make such evaluations public. As the Education Code states, I most certainly do have the right to order you not to distribute matters dealing with Phillips personnel to anyone outside the school."

It was a hard stand—I'll give him that. But Jack's defiance had resurrected the spirit of our group, and I believe that just then everyone in the room recognized that at the very least our adversary had blinked.

Nor was he done blinking. "Let me repeat my earlier point," Laws said. "I do not oppose the idea of evaluating administrators. In fact, let me make you an offer right now." Here he flipped a couple of pages ahead and began reading again: "'Let us organize a committee together to draw up a more equitable evaluation form.'"

Questioning looks flew around the cafeteria.

"All I ask," Laws said, "is that we include some teachers who were not involved in creating the current documents. That way we can begin the process free from prejudice."

Jack raised his tufted eyebrows and winked at me. The principal's intent was clear: He aimed at moving forward only after slapping down the perceived architects of the nefarious scheme.

As soon as I saw the majority of my colleagues nodding in agreement with Laws's suggestion, I realized that Jack's plan was doomed. The principal's proposal sounded reasonable enough to most all of them—even to Betty Warden, and she generally saw through such diversions. Obviously, the faculty thought the purpose of this meeting had more to do with Corny Whittaker's desire for fairness than with the state of the Phillips union chapter.

It was Roland Swett who blew up at the compromise. "I will not be the target of a witch hunt," he exclaimed, spittle on his lips, gray hair awry. "I won't have my career ruined by some wild, antagonistic, non-thinking—" he stopped as if searching for the most appropriately degrading epithet with which to trash us "—teachers!" he finally blurted out.

At that moment the bell rang. The school day was about to begin. We, the opposition, were left no time to rebut. Vivian Laws had properly planned the length of his presentation. As we prepared to leave for our classrooms, it felt like those of us who showed up in the cafeteria had put our heads into a collective noose.

"Why fight it?" Frick said to me on our way out the door. "I never considered Jack's plan such a great idea in the first place, and the old man did agree to the general idea of being evaluated. That's a victory in itself, don't you think? What's so terrible about forming a committee like the one he was talking about?"

Clearly, nothing—at least, not to Frick and those who thought like him.

🎓

Laws's new group met the following week. As expected, I wasn't a member; neither was Jack. When the revised evaluation forms appeared on the very last day of the fall semester, they looked surprisingly like those that Jack himself had designed—except for one detail. There were still the three columns to be completed next to each character trait; the first two boxes, the ones titled "Excellent" and "Satisfactory," remained the same. It was only the third that had been altered. Laws had replaced the small box for "Unsatisfactory" with a much wider space now labeled much less critically. The word, "Comments," headed the third column.

"It isn't a complete disaster," Mandy reassured me when the time came a week or two later to complete the anonymous forms. "People can still write their most heartfelt thoughts; they still have the chance to protest if they want."

Mandy, who still resented Laws's view of her teaching skills, was right, of course—even though she herself had no plans to write a diatribe against the man. For that matter, no realistic teacher on the

Phillips faculty had any serious expectations that anything would result from those forms, that any written comments from teachers might actually serve to undermine the authority of the school's administration.

Needless to say, the completed forms never left the principal's office.

Chapter Nine

The New Semester

*V*ivian Laws's success in undermining the evaluation controversy marked another turning point for me. Prior to the appearance of the alternative forms, I had avoided the idea of cajoling or coercing people to take an active part in union business. Let people do what they want, I figured. Persuasion was more in Jack's line.

It was just such a cautionary approach that had prompted me to counsel moderation in Mandy's response to the principal's unfair evaluation of her teaching. But once I witnessed Laws so disdainfully dismissing the desires of so many of my colleagues, I began to think differently.

In spite of my earlier lack of faith in our faculty, I did encounter a few others who saw through Laws's charade. In her Southern drawl, Sarah Mertz summed up the principal's strategy this way: "Our Mr. Laws is no gentleman." Randy Stones called him an asshole.

But for the passive majority who simply seemed annoyed, I sensed the need for a more dramatic approach. To most of the teachers at

Phillips, traditional union tactics seemed like nonstarters—leafleting parents with our discontent, too extreme; boycotting faculty meetings, too radical; and withholding grades until we gained some sort of satisfaction, clearly unfair to the kids as well as a breach of our legal responsibilities.

Just when I feared I'd run out of options, I got lucky. According to union officials, the ongoing negotiations with the school district over salary raises and working conditions had reached a stalemate. By late January, Los Angeles radio and TV news broadcasts about the possibility of teacher walkouts and strikes were vying for attention with reports of the countrywide turmoil concerning the Vietnam War.

The current Gallup Poll showed that 65% of Americans supported President Nixon's handling of the war, yet television-news producers recognized that they could enlarge their local audiences with stories concerning labor unrest in the school district. After all, parents watched TV too. Accounts of low teacher salaries, large class sizes, and questionable labor practices affected families throughout Los Angeles. So when strike-related interviews with union leaders appeared on the screen and school-district officials steadfastly maintained that no work stoppage was expected, viewers paid attention.

Teachers had no idea how the situation would resolve itself. Though I hadn't taken an official survey of the Phillips faculty, I recognized that morally and financially, you should never minimize the effects of a strike. No matter what one's position on the societal ladder, if a strike lasts too long and workers lose enough salary, the results can be devastating. To counteract such fears, some unions have their members contribute in advance to a strike fund, but the Los Angeles teachers' union isn't one of them. And yet I'd heard enough grumbling from a small number of my colleagues to suspect that not even the threat of monetary loss could dissuade them from the chance of sticking it to our principal.

Political protests continued to roil the country; the spirit of dissent permeated the atmosphere. As a consequence, the more possible I believed a teachers' strike in Los Angeles to be, a city-wide teachers' strike that just might stoke enough courage and offer enough cover to our own faculty to shut down Phillips. Flexing our union muscle might be the very thing to unite the faculty. In fact, with the collective power of the city's more than twenty thousand teachers behind us, I felt we couldn't lose.

"And exactly what do you intend to say?" Vivian Laws asked me, his voice hard and unyielding. I had just told him I wanted some speaking time at the first faculty meeting of the new semester, and he wasn't happy about it. "I can't have you offering up subversive comments like those anti-war beatniks," he said. "How often is this going to happen, this call for walkouts—at every meeting until you people get what you want?"

"You people," I thought—as if somehow teachers and administrators weren't all in this together. Though what I actually said was, "Mr. Laws, the board has agreed that the union representative has the right to speak at faculty meetings."

"But not to advocate walking out of schools," the principal said, "not to advocate breaking the law."

"I'm only going to tell everybody about the ballots they'll be getting in the mail, sir. Nothing more."

Too savvy to contradict a school board directive, the principal agreed to let me speak. He really had no choice.

I was already pumped up when I'd joined Mandy and Jack in the library for Tuesday's after-school meeting. With all the strike-talk going on, I was pretty sure that on this occasion, unlike the initial meeting the previous September, people would actually listen to me. A teacher walkout concerned everyone.

What's more, thanks to the close-minded approach Laws had taken regarding the evaluation controversy, not only did I feel the power of the city's teachers behind me, but I also felt fairly confident that I would be speaking on behalf of the majority of my Phillips colleagues.

Laws too must have recognized the faculty's newfound skepticism, for he began the meeting with a reference to the selfsame evaluation controversy. "Last semester," he said, slowly rocking back and forth at the podium, "a few of you wrote evaluations of me and my staff. Report cards, if you will. For the most part, the assessments were constructive, although apparently—" he paused to offer a brief chuckle "—I do have a few critics out there."

Union Jack was one of them. He told me how he'd used a black marker to convert the section of the new forms titled "Comments" back to its original "unsatisfactory" designation. Then on Laws's form, he marked "unsat" all the way down the page. I just wrote the letter "U" in all the comment sections; Mandy didn't turn hers in.

"Before we get to today's business," the principal said. "I'd like to welcome aboard a new member of the faculty—history teacher Harry Barnes."

Laws gestured towards his right where a bespectacled young man in suit and tie half rose in his seat and smiled sheepishly at his new colleagues. There was a brief clapping of hands; and Barnes, who looked about twenty-five, responded with a self-conscious smile and a pat of his brown hair before sitting down again. He seemed nice enough.

"Mr. Barnes is a true beginner," Laws explained. "Today is his very first day of teaching."

Additional applause, a bit more energetic.

"A brand-new teacher," Mandy whispered to me. "I guess I have seniority over someone."

"You gain and you lose," the principal said. "We've gained Mr. Barnes, but we've lost Mrs. Whittaker—at least for a while."

I joined my colleagues in scanning the room. Even though personnel changes occur at schools all the time, you don't think that someone's no longer around just because you haven't spotted them. Then again, schools are transient places. In addition to the teachers that everyone's heard about—the legendary characters who (for better or worse) remain at an institution for decades—there are always many more who frequently move about. In a profession in which half its members quit within their first five years, most non-teachers don't realize how much instability there is on a school's faculty and how much time is spent in training new people.

Yet nobody really believed that a mainstay like Corny Whittaker could actually be gone. On this day, you figured she was simply not in attendance.

"I've been told," Laws said, "that Mrs. Whittaker had a minor accident at her home."

Jack leaned over to us. "Corny broke her leg Friday night," he said quietly. "She called to tell me. She slipped on the stairs at her house."

"Obviously," Laws went on, "Mrs. Whittaker will be sorely missed. We hope for her quick recovery."

Jack made no effort to hide his sneer.

"At this late date," the principal said, pointing to the front row of teachers, "we're fortunate enough to get a veteran back to sub for us, so our girls can continue their home-ec classes."

A tiny, grey-haired woman sitting close to the podium raised a shaky hand. Her students probably thought she was close to a hundred.

For the rest of the hour, Laws and his cohorts spelled out the usual concerns for the start of the new semester. Only after the administrators had finished reviewing the same procedures most of us could recite by heart did Laws get around to announcing it was time for union business.

"Before Mr. Malamud speaks," he said, his tone developing a harder edge, "let me conclude with a few words of my own regarding the so-called job-action or strike—I'm not afraid to use the word—advocated by the teachers' union. Understand that I'm not anti-organization. But I do believe in this 'good ship Phillips,' and, quite frankly, I don't want to see it blown full of holes. You should all know," Laws said, raising his right hand as if swearing on a Bible, "that if there is a walkout, we, your administrators, are prepared to pick up the pieces and run with the ball."

I was still frowning at the mixed metaphor when Laws waved me up to the microphone. Slowly, I made my way between the tables to the front of the room.

"Be very careful," Laws whispered when I reached the podium. Only then did he take a step back.

A sea of faces regarded me expectantly, and in my strongest teacher-voice I presented the facts. "Mr. Laws has mentioned a possible strike. Rest assured, there will be no such action unless we vote to have one."

"Shut it down!" Betty Warden cried out. With a scowling Vivian Laws only twenty feet away, it was quite a show of defiance.

"The union wants me to tell you," I said, "that within the next couple of months—probably sometime in March—all our members will be receiving ballots in the mail along with a union brief on the pros and cons of walking out. The ballots will contain a simple yes-or-no question: Do you want to strike against the school district?"

Suddenly, Nate Fodor, the usually silent print-shop teacher, spoke up. "If you plan to walk out, people," he proclaimed in his solid bass voice, "be ready to stay out."

Jack raised his fist in support, and a few others clapped their confirmation.

Laws was standing directly behind me, so it took him but a moment to recapture the mic. "This is not a political rally," he growled, glaring at me as if I had just incited an assault on the Pentagon. Then he aimed his menacing glare at the unfortunates in the front row, and the faculty grew silent again.

I couldn't say exactly how much of my enthusiasm was triggered by revenge; but as I surveyed the sullen features of my colleagues, I figured that a whole lot of people sitting in the library that afternoon were feeling the same way.

At the start of the new semester, I opened my ninth-grade classes with a unit on creative writing. I asked the kids to compose a list of familiar workers preceded by the stereotypical adjectives usually associated with the role— "graceful ballerina," for instance, or "brave soldier." Then I had them rewrite the two columns while inverting the workers' list so that each adjective no longer appeared with its traditional mate. As might be expected, the results produced provocative combinations like "brave ballerina" or "graceful soldier." Finally, I challenged the kids to write fictional character sketches about their weirdest pairing.

For Mandy, the second semester offered the opportunity not only to rework any rookie mistakes, but also to face her kids with the new insights she'd gained. She took full advantage. In fact, you could chart her success by listening to her students. The first semester there'd been little chatter. Now, I was hearing about the "cool history teacher with the red hair"— "cool" remaining the highest accolade a teacher can earn. I could only hope that so many encouraging compliments would help her forget the unwarranted evaluation she'd received from Laws back in December.

If spending more of our non-teaching hours together was any indication, such seemed to be the case. After grading papers, we'd frequently go out to dinner and a movie—at least, on weekends. One Sunday we went to the Griffith Observatory, and a week later we took in a ballgame at Dodger Stadium.

On another weekend we drove out to Disneyland. From loving the Magic Kingdom to protesting the war in Vietnam, Mandy and I seemed to concur on just about everything during those weekend excursions—everything except school politics in general and the looming strike in particular.

"Socially acceptable payback," she said one rainy night on our way to my apartment. "That's all the strike is." We were driving down a drenched Olympic after burgers and fries at the Hamlet on Sunset, and I had mentioned something about expecting the Phillips faculty to vote in favor of the walkout. "For you," she said, "it's all about getting back at Laws."

"Maybe it is," I said, squinting into the dark, wet street ahead. "But however personal it might be for me, that doesn't absolve you from making a decision. You're part of the faculty. One way or another, you're going to have to take some sort of stand."

Fat drops of water exploded in slow motion on the windshield. The robotic wipers brushed them away to make room for a new barrage an instant later—a symbol of our bickering on the subject, I thought.

We remained silent. Headlights reflected off the pavement as we drove along in the rain.

"You know," I said at last, "you're not going to get me to change my mind."

"Who even wants to?"

"I'm still voting to walk out."

"And what about your draft deferment?"

My deferment. I had to confess, like most of Mandy's views, it was a practical consideration and one which I'd chosen not to think much about. The First Amendment might guarantee your right to strike, but walking a picket line's not an activity destined to keep you out of the army, especially during a war.

"Look," I said, "I admit that I originally became union rep to help Jack out."

"Nice," she replied, "but nothing politically noble."

"You're right. But I wouldn't have taken the job if I hadn't believed in the philosophy behind it. So now it's on me. Deferment or not, if there's a strike, I'm the one who's going to lead our faculty out the door. I'm the union rep; it's my responsibility."

Mandy settled her left hand against the back of my neck and began massaging it to the accompaniment of the wipers. "I do respect your conviction," she said.

Mandy's accusation of payback notwithstanding, I felt certain that she agreed with me, that only the precariousness of her first-year position was stopping her from joining in. I'd reacted much the same way back in Berkeley when I didn't feel independent enough—or maybe even brave enough—to join the free-speech protests.

Like Mandy's defense of her first-year vulnerability, there was truth in my college justification—that business about being at school on my folks' dime and not having the right to throw away their investment. But if I was being honest, I would have to admit that such an argument was also protective cover.

"You know I sympathize with you," Mandy said, the rain splattering down even harder as we turned left from Olympic. "It's just that walking out is something I don't feel comfortable doing. Especially with that evaluation from Laws still in my mind. It's my first year, Art. Maybe I'm just a little bit scared."

We pulled up in front of Mrs. Gross's building, and I shut off the engine. From the street, you couldn't see my small place in the back. Despite the darkness, a nearby lamppost lit up the two turrets of the front apartments, and in the rain they seemed to shimmer. Through the wet windshield, the streetlight illuminated Mandy's face, and the reflected water inching down the glass appeared on her cheeks like falling tears.

And yet, the gleam in her green eyes told a different story. "I have made up my mind about one thing," she said. "I am going to join the union. It's the least I can do."

"Really?"

"It doesn't mean that I'll strike, but it does mean that I am officially on your side."

I hugged her in appreciation.

"Just don't tell my dad," she whispered.

For a few more minutes we sat out front in the car listening to the water splash down. On the radio came a report about the convictions in the trial of the Chicago Seven, the anti-war protestors charged with crossing state lines to incite a riot at the 1968 Democratic National Convention. With our own possible strike not far off, I worried that the guilty verdicts might be an omen—the inevitable consequence of messing with the establishment. As the Dart's windshield steamed up and the globe of the streetlight transformed into a bright but amorphous blur, I wondered if we teachers were foolish to expect anything better.

During the first two months of the spring term, evolving political issues, both national and local, vied for attention. The United States expanded America's presence in Vietnam to include Cambodia. As a consequence, the percentage of support for Nixon's handling of the war dropped from the sixties into the forties. Around the country people were questioning authority. In Los Angeles the public began to doubt assurances from the school board that there was little possibility of a teachers' strike.

Weekend dinners and movies helped distract Mandy and me from the tumult, but it was the daily routine of our jobs that truly enabled us to move on. I continued my unit on creative writing by assigning classes a number of short stories that served as models before they wrote their own. Pieces by Shirley Jackson and Guy de Maupassant were among the favorites. I love the outrage when the kids learn that the protagonist in Maupassant's "The Necklace" has ruined her life by paying for a lost necklace she thinks is worth a fortune, but which turns out to be fake. Or when they discover what ending up "the winner" really means in Jackson's "The Lottery."

At the same time, Mandy was teaching her eighth-grade classes about the Spanish-American War. To dramatize the impact of William Randolph Hearst's sensationalized "yellow journalism," she had her students use yellow construction paper to create a jingoistic newspaper about the war. With so dramatic an approach, it seemed a lucky break for Mandy that Mrs. Steele had chosen to observe the lesson in which Mandy was handing out such relevant topics as the blowing up of the American battle ship *Maine* in Havana Harbor and the heroic charge of Teddy Roosevelt's Rough Riders up San Juan Hill.

In the contemporary world, reporters like Hersh of My Lai Massacre fame were digging for hidden facts behind the Vietnam War, and Mrs. Steele should have appreciated how Mandy was linking the historical past to our immediate present. Instead, all the vice-principal had to say to her about the lesson was, "Interesting, I'm sure, but the study of newspapers really belongs in the English class."

Ask any teacher: Your initial year in front of a room full of kids is a challenge and a grind. You're reading new textbooks, plotting new class calendars, learning new classroom-management skills. Novices can use all the help they can get, all the positive reinforcement; and yet however obvious the observation, the importance of a teacher's first year is a fact that the administrators at Phillips seemed determined to ignore.

By the end of March, the strike ballots went out in the mail, and despite my specific worries about Mandy, more general matters beckoned. Teaching went on, of course, but political issues loomed large. Basically, the futures of all the teachers in Los Angeles hung in the balance, and while we busied ourselves with our routines, the outcome of the strike-vote occupied most all of our thinking.

On a Friday afternoon in early April, the union announced the results of the balloting. In the spirit of the anti-war protests sweeping the country, teachers throughout the Los Angeles school district had voted two-to-one to approve the walkout; and just like that, practicalities dominated my life. Picket signs. Telephone trees. Food supplies. Donations. Communications. Not to mention the recruitment of participants.

On the night the results were announced, Mandy had suggested Madame Wu's in Santa Monica for dinner. As soon as we had gotten into the car, however, she warned, "Don't ask me again because I will not strike," and my enthusiasm for the meal ebbed. Driving west down Wilshire, I didn't say a word.

My reticence lasted until a few blocks past 26th Street, just before we pulled into the parking lot. "You do have to remember," I felt compelled to remind her, "that if you go in to work, that if you cross the picket line, the striking teachers, your colleagues, will call you a scab."

"Sticks and stones," she said. "Let's go eat."

I parked the car, and soon we were sitting at a small table watching our waiter spoon sizzling-rice into a steaming broth. Mandy frowned as the rice began to crackle. "I think you know how torn I feel," she said once the waiter had left. "Everything tells me I belong outside the school. But like I said the other night, I feel too vulnerable as a first-year-teacher."

"Sometimes you have to take a risk," I said, not knowing what else to tell her. "That's what I did when I agreed to be the union rep."

She took both my hands in hers. "But you had years to prepare, Art. I'm still new at this. You've been listening to that nonsense from Laws a lot longer than I have. And you've had the wisdom of 'Union Jack' to guide you through it all. Maybe I need more time."

"The strike starts Monday," I said. "You don't have a lot of time left."

We said very little to each other during the rest of our dinner.

Chapter Ten

The Strike

*O*n a chilly Monday morning in mid-April, the walkout began. To the doomsayers, the overcast sky might have seemed an inauspicious start. Yet any Angeleno can tell you that during the spring, the early marine layer that blocks the sun generally burns off by mid-morning and blue skies follow.

Before setting off for school, I checked and rechecked the last-minute details I needed to take care of—positioning our picketers, reviewing union bulletins, and loading into my car a stack of "On Strike" picket signs printed by the union. For myself, I brought along the sign I created: It featured a large photo of Mark Twain alongside one of my favorite Twain aphorisms: "In the first place, God made idiots. This was for practice. Then he made school boards."

Such tasks diverted my anxiety. As long as I was dealing with practicalities I could avoid thinking about my upcoming encounter with Mandy. I could avoid picturing our face-to-face confrontation on the picket line. I could avoid wondering how I was going to react if she really did walk past me.

The closer I got to school, the more the logistics of the strike took over. Mainly, I thought about how many teachers would be walking out. Though lots of them had promised, Jack warned that as with any political demonstration, you can never be certain which people turn out until you actually see them pounding the pavement.

The question of who would show up occupied my thoughts as I drove faster than usual past the large white houses, broad emerald lawns, and leafy ficus trees that filled the neighborhood surrounding Phillips. The sooner I got to school, the sooner I'd know the size of the picket line. Only when I reached the front of the building did I slow down.

Despite the morning gloom, the large brass letters that spelled out DAVID GRAHAM PHILLIPS JUNIOR HIGH SCHOOL above the red double-doors of the entrance looked particularly shiny. It was a handsome scene, but it was devoid of people. In particular, it was devoid of striking teachers. The wide walkway leading to the main entrance was empty. So was the sidewalk that ran the length of the building. I held my breath. Where was everyone?

Just then, Jack and Betty turned the corner and paraded into my vision. I could relax. Moments later, Penelope Martinez, Tiffany Schwartz, and Sam Turner came walking towards me from the other direction, with new teacher Harry Barnes hurrying to catch up. I could go park the Dart.

Seeking distance between my car and the school, I pulled over beneath a sycamore tree a good half-block away. With the Dart serving as Command Central, I figured there was no need to provide Vivian Laws the opportunity to survey our union activities from his office window. Even though he kept the blinds closed, it was easy to imagine him peering through the slats.

Once out of the car, I began stacking the picket signs next to a neatly-manicured parkway. Jack came over to help, handing out signs to new arrivals as well as to those already marching in front of the school. With each new striker, I grew more pleased and, checking the notes I'd made earlier, suggested where people should do their walking. I sent a few picketers to the lampposts at the end of the walkway, some towards the faculty parking lot, and everyone else spread out along the sidewalk at the front of the school.

"Where's Jeremy?" I asked Betty when she strolled by.

"He's over at Whitman High. He's been subbing there a lot and thought he should be striking with his brothers and sisters. Union solidarity and all that, you know." She pointed her sign at Jack. "I'll hang out with you," she told him.

Most of the teachers were carrying the union placards Jack had given them. But just as I'd done, some others had created signs of their own. One proclaimed, "Teachers Have Class"; another, "If You Can Read This, Thank a Teacher."

It was still early, and the neighborhood hadn't fully awakened when a red Ford station wagon came barreling down the road. Corny Whittaker pulled up to the curb just a few feet from the path to the main entrance. Due to her bad leg, she hadn't been allowed back to teach, but here she was on the first day of the strike ready to walk. Enveloped in a heavy green coat and black slacks, she swiveled out of the driver's seat and stood with the aid of a wooden cane.

Jack led a cluster of colleagues to her car to welcome her. By the time I joined the group, she was in mid-story: ". . . so I asked if I could have the sewing machines moved to a room on the ground floor. I wanted to be able to get to my classes without climbing the stairs. You know, because of my leg." She raised the cane for emphasis. "But all Mr. Laws said was, 'If you're not ready to teach on the second floor, then you're not ready to teach.'"

"What a shit," somebody muttered.

"I don't know," Corny frowned. "Maybe, he really was trying to protect me from hurting myself."

"Well, we're just glad you're here, Corny," I said. She seemed to have overcome her unnerving experience with Laws and his evaluations-related threat—unless, of course, it was that very episode that had prompted her to join the strike.

"Oh, I almost forgot," she said, tapping her forehead with the rounded handle of the cane, "I brought goodies."

With the help of her cane, she limped towards the rear of the Ford and opened the red tailgate. It was one of those horizontal half-doors that pull down like a hinged table. Inside, an early-morning treasure greeted us—three shopping bags filled with dozens of golden bagels and small, silver tubs of cream cheese; three tall thermoses of coffee; and four flat, white boxes that turned out to be loaded with doughnuts, both chocolate and glazed.

Slowly, she swept her arm over the food. "My contribution to the strike," she said. "I can certainly walk well enough to go shopping, and—" here she raised her voice in the direction of the school building "—I hope Mr. Laws can hear me." Then she spread a red-plaid tablecloth on top of the fold-down door. Arranging the food as if we were at a picnic brought more teachers by.

"Thanks, Corny," I said, dodging people's attempts to grab a coffee or doughnut. "Much appreciated." My own move towards the food, however, was cut short by a shout from Jack.

"Here they come." He was pointing up the street where a caravan of three cars was heading for the teachers' parking lot. A few picketers were already marching near the driveway; the rest of us, signs held high, hurried back onto the sidewalk to welcome the scabs personally.

Outrage drowned all my political righteousness as I watched Don Frick maneuver his restored, dark-blue '34 Pontiac past the picketers and into the lot. Randy Stones and math teacher Martin

Osaka closely followed, Stones in a new black Chevy truck and Osaka in a light-blue '57 Thunderbird. Though I expected such confrontations, they were still hard to process. These were people we'd been working with just the previous week, people we'd been breaking bread with for years—people we'd partied with—and here they were, driving past their striking colleagues as if we were invisible.

On normal school days, teachers would walk from the parking lot up the sidewalk to the front of the school. But since that was the place where most of us were now marching, it was not surprising to watch Stones and Osaka, who I am sure sought no confrontation with the strikers, dodge all of us by cutting through the rear of the campus and entering the building via a back door near the gym.

Not Don Frick. He marched straight towards us. Far from avoiding the picket line, the little woodshop teacher grinned at everybody. When he reached the lampposts at the top of the path, he turned to me. "Good morning," he said. Before striding up the walkway, he extended his middle finger. "Have a nice day."

I glared back at him with as stern a "teacher look" as I could muster. It must have had some impact, for I watched with satisfaction as his grin dissolved into a child-like look of embarrassment.

I had no time to relish my success, however, for no sooner had Frick turned away than I saw Mandy's white Beetle enter the parking lot. She was probably too far away to have seen Frick's little display; or perhaps Mrs. Nichols, the librarian, who was just then hurrying towards the walkway, had blocked our encounter. In one hand, she carried a large canvas-bag full of books while with the other she secured her old-fashioned straw hat atop her head. As she hustled up the path, the small clusters of red and yellow wax fruit attached to the large-brim bobbed up and down.

Teachers, kids, parents—all sorts of people were filling the sidewalk now, yet I simply stopped and stared into the parking lot. I watched Mandy get out of her car, lock it, and with bookbag on shoulder walk slowly towards the sidewalk. She paused for a moment at the gate and looked up and down the block.

Only after seeing the striking teachers in front of the school did she begin to head slowly up the street in our direction. From her first move out of the car, she had looked uncomfortable. She'd taken a couple of steps forward, halted, then started off again. At one point just beyond the parking-lot gate, she paused to shift her bag from her right shoulder to her left, disentangling some strands of her red hair from the bag's strap in the process. You didn't need to watch too carefully to note that the closer she got, the more her pace slackened.

As I'd discovered minutes before, some people can brush right past their friends and co-workers without a second thought. Yet from the start, I really didn't think Mandy was one of them. Deep down, I just couldn't believe that she'd actually turn her back on Betty or Corny or Jack. Or me. That's why I wasn't totally surprised when she stopped, did an about-face, and hurried back to the parking lot.

I suppose she might have forgotten something in her car. Or maybe she'd been shamed into going home. But when she pulled the Beetle out of the lot and proceeded to find a place to park down the street, I realized that she understood that you can't leave your car on the premises of the organization you're striking against.

This time after she got out of the Beetle, she walked directly towards us with no book bag on her shoulder. A large group of picketers joined me in staring at her, for Mandy had become the first teacher who'd actually turned around at the sight of our picket line, the first teacher that we had collectively dissuaded from going to work.

"You win," was all she said to me.

The teachers who were close enough to hear applauded. Sarah Mertz handed her a picket sign. It read, "The Board Giveth and the Board Taketh Away."

Our students buzzed with energy. Thrilled at the prospect of empty classrooms and seeing their teachers hoisting picket signs up and down the block, the kids crowded around us, asking all sorts of questions.

"How long'll you be on strike?"

"Does this mean no homework?"

"You gonna be on the news?"

We answered as best we could.

"We don't know how long the strike will last."

"You have to do the work the teachers inside assign you."

"Watch the news to learn more about what's going on."

Then we did our best to hustle the kids into the building. After all, that's where they belonged. It also didn't hurt that the more kids there were inside, the greater the challenge for an understaffed faculty to oversee any kind of conventional learning.

The bell that announced the start of the school day also marked the end of most all of the pedestrian traffic. Oh, there were the few kids who arrived late and had to scurry into the building; but once classes began, it was only the striking teachers who commandeered the long sidewalk in front of the school.

Fittingly enough in a nation at war, each school day began with a recording on the P.A. system of the military bugle-refrain, "To the Colors." While it played, students who'd been selected in advance by the principal raised the American flag in the courtyard behind the main building. Everywhere on campus, faculty and students were supposed to stop whatever they were doing and stand at respectful attention until the ritual ended. Those of us out on the street paused as well.

Once I saw that the flag was flying, I signaled the picketers to re-converge at Corny's car. Within minutes some thirty teachers made their way from their various positions along the sidewalk and were soon drinking coffee and gobbling up doughnuts and bagels.

I myself had just picked up a bagel when I saw Jack flick his head in the direction of the school. Vivian Laws and Roland Swett were standing in front of the red doors like two generals surveying the battlefield—no doubt, like all the other principals throughout the city, taking a headcount for the district of the number of strikers outside the building.

While I could only wonder what the board was going to do to us, I watched Laws mumble something to the vice-principal and point in our direction. In response, Roland Swett marched down the concrete path to Corny's red Ford.

By the time he reached us, the gray old man was trying to catch his breath. "Mr. Laws," he said to no one in particular, "wants whoever owns this car to move it. You people are making too much noise. We can't conduct classes inside."

"Classes?" Betty Warden laughed. "Who are you trying to kid? You can't conduct classes because you don't have enough teachers. We're all out here. Just look around."

As she spoke, more strikers joined the group, and voices of support chimed in. "Right." "Yeah."

Swett's face turned red. "I told you to move the car," he said again.

With her outstretched cane pointing the way, Corny Whittaker parted the crowd and limped slowly towards the vice-principal. It was her station wagon, and his demand was suggesting that the homemaking teacher repeal her hospitality. Swett actually backed up as Corny, her great green coat furnishing added bulk, stretched as tall as her wooden cane would allow. "This car moves," she proclaimed, "over my dead body."

Swett's mouth formed a small circle of surprise. After all, as a vice-principal, he was the personification of the school district's power. Or was supposed to be.

We stared in amazement at Corny's bravado.

"You go, girl," Mandy said.

For his part, Roland Swett turned around and retreated up the walkway.

"Chalk one up for the good guys," Jack crowed and put his arm around Corny.

I waved my bagel at the homemaking teacher as a kind of salute to our first-day's hero. Right then, the sun began to burn its way through the clouds.

By the end of the first week of the strike, we had established a daily routine. Teachers arrived early enough to confront the scabs and then, once school had begun, congregated at Corny's station wagon to feast on the breakfast she provided. I did my best to collect enough money from everyone so we could reimburse her, but since she was always finding new delicacies to bring us—French crullers one day, Mexican churros the next—I can't be sure we ever paid her in full.

The first week bled into the second, and our activities expanded. One afternoon we attended a pep rally at a neighborhood movie theater rented by the union. On another occasion, we picketed a nearby elementary school, joining its striking faculty in a display of union solidarity. All the while, we had to tolerate our share of indignities. "Communists!" some wag shouted from a passing car. "Strike on weekends!" shouted another.

Well into the second week, our picket line remained strong. We had only one defection. On the second Monday of the walkout, Nate Fodor, the print-shop teacher with the deep voice, the same Nate Fodor who'd told everyone planning to strike that they'd better be prepared to stay out for the duration, crossed the picket line and went back to work. People said he was particularly afraid of losing his health benefits—as if the rest of us weren't.

No matter the day's activity, however, we always made it our business to return to Phillips in time to wave good-bye to our colleagues who continued to work inside. By our estimates, they made up less than half the faculty.

And Phillips typified Los Angeles as a whole. Over fifty-percent of all the teachers in the city had walked off their jobs. Despite school district propaganda to the contrary, you can't run an educational program when you're missing more than half your staff. The union maintained that virtually every school in the district would have shut down if the decision had been left to the principals, and no doubt the union was right.

With the pay of administrators tied to that of teachers, the board feared that some principals would side with the strikers and close their schools with the hope of ultimately raising their own salaries. Reducing the power of the principals would minimize such an occurrence; so, to the surprise of no one, the district removed from principals the authority to shut individual campuses.

Such a decision typified the school board's top-down, military-style thinking. It represented the main reason teachers continue to call district headquarters "The Fort." While rumors suggest that the nickname can claim some historical basis—the original building was said to have been constructed on the site of an old army garrison—most teachers relate the name to the kind of dictatorial strategizing that goes on inside the place. Indeed, many considered it oddly prophetic when the district recently hired a retired military officer to serve as superintendent.

Though we ignored our professional obligation to come to work, we took most seriously the union's warning to keep kids safe and out of our picket lines, and we passed along the admonition to our students. But hoping to keep close to the action, the kids found any number of ways to help us.

At exactly 10:02 in the middle of the strike's second week, for instance, all of the windows in the ground-floor classrooms flew open; and like some sort of premeditated sneak-evacuation, hundreds of students in all shapes and sizes came tumbling out of the windows and onto the front lawn. Within minutes, they gathered on the sidewalk across the street from us and set up their own picket line in sympathy with their striking teachers.

Even some of the kids who stayed away from school got into the action by encouraging their parents to invite the striking teachers home for lunch. I can't speak for schools in other neighborhoods; but fortunately for us, the large houses surrounding Phillips feature expansive backyards. During the strike, groups of parents got together and laid out fixings like cold cuts and bread and fruit and cookies, and we teachers lined up with paper plates, collected our meals, and enjoyed scenic lunches amid fountains and gardens.

If and when any of the kids from the families that hosted those luncheons returned to school, they would meet us on the picket line and report how Mr. Laws had grilled them. He would ask how many teachers had showed up for lunch, who they were, and did any of them know how long the strike was supposed to last.

🎓

Maintaining the picket line kept me busy; but thanks to our daily routine, I spent less of my time worrying about where everybody was than I'd done at the start of the strike. Unimpeded by tactical concerns, I returned to thinking about my relationship with Mandy. Winter break had convinced me how much I wanted us to be together. The occasional evening meal after school, the all-too-brief weekends, the joint walks on the picket line—none of it was enough.

I wanted Mandy to move in with me. There was room in my place—more than in hers anyway. We'd known each other since September, and it was now late April. Some high-minded moralists might argue that eight months isn't enough time for anybody to make so serious a decision. All I can say is that it felt right to me.

During the buildup to the strike, I'd put off asking Mandy about her feelings on the subject. But now that political matters had settled down and the two of us were walking the line day after day, I thought about little else than how sweet our living together would be. I imagined—or, at least, hoped— she felt the same.

"It'd be so much simpler if we drove to school in the same car," I said to her one morning beneath our picket signs. She'd pulled up in her VW again, and I was counting on the logic of my argument to win her over. "We'd see each other sooner if we did."

"Of course, we would," she said, eyeing me suspiciously, "especially, if we woke up together—if that's what you're getting at."

"Can't fool you," I laughed. "We'd have a lot more fun. And since I live closer to Phillips than you do, we'd save on gas."

"Ah," Mandy nodded, "the practical approach."

"That's right," I said, gaining confidence. After all, she hadn't rejected the idea. "And while we're on the subject of practicality, think how much money you'll be saving on rent if we're just splitting mine."

She didn't laugh; she didn't even smile. "I don't know, Art. We haven't known each other that long—"

"Almost nine months," I said with what I intended to sound like matter-of-fact finality, like what was so wrong with that?

"—and people will talk when they see us arriving together. Is our private life something we want Mr. Laws to know about?"

I was prepared for that argument, especially since Mandy had used it before the Christmas party. "If Laws even cares, we can tell him—and anyone else who asks—that we carpool. And it'd be the truth."

"I suppose it would save on gas," she said sarcastically. But then she got serious again. "You know I want to be with you. But what if my dad finds out? I told you he's kind of conservative."

"I've thought of that too," I said. "You could hang on to your apartment for a while. You'd still be paying rent, but it'll give us an escape hatch. If things don't work out, you'll have somewhere to go back to. Your mail would keep going there anyway, and you could pick it up every few days."

"But my dad—"

"That's the point. He'll never know the difference."

"What if he calls?"

"I admit that's a problem. But, hey, you can tell him you were out."

"Easy for you to say. I just hope he doesn't call too often—or too late at night."

"Come on, Mandy. Keeping your place won't be for long. After we're all set and you give it up, you can tell your dad that in order to save money you got a new apartment with a roommate."

"I don't know," she said again. Then she stopped walking and—right out there on the picket line—gently laid her hand on my cheek. "This is a big step, Art. As much as it sounds like a good idea, you've got to let me think about it some more."

I nodded, more than a bit disappointed. But at the very least, I'd shared with her my intentions.

In the middle of the third week of the strike, shocking news related to the war in Southeast Asia—only this time, closer to home—overshadowed our walkout. During a demonstration on May 4 to protest America's advancement into Cambodia, four college students at Ohio's Kent State University were shot and killed by the National Guard.

As a consequence, in a more real way than ever before, I imagined that most of us on our own picket line contemplated the consequences of political protest. I'm sure that nobody believed we were in mortal danger, but then probably neither did the four dead and nine wounded students at Kent State. Suffice it to say that the last issue I wanted to deal with on that fateful day was the ear-piercing blare of a car horn.

Yet duty called. The blast came from Don Frick's classic Pontiac, and it heralded the first major conflict on the picket line. School had ended for the day, and the initial rush of kids had dissipated. As usual, Jack and Betty were marching back and forth across the driveway of the faculty parking lot as the scabs were beginning to leave. But on this day, perhaps motivated by their anger at what had occurred at Kent State, they decided that rather than backing off, they'd slow their pace and delay the flow of cars trying to exit.

The first few drivers waited patiently for the two strikers to get out of the way and allow them to drive out. But not Don Frick. He had no intention of just sitting there. Jack and Betty were crossing the driveway when he reached the front of the line, and Frick slammed the heel of his hand down hard on the horn of his ancient Pontiac—slammed it down so hard that the horn stuck.

Mandy and I stopped walking and stared at the old car. At the same time, even with the wail of the horn, I could hear the clatter of heels rapidly approaching from behind. I didn't know to whom they belonged, but from the quick staccato beat I knew there was going to be trouble. When I did turn around, I saw the stern face of Tiffany Schwartz bearing down on me, her silver hair bouncing on her shoulders, the wood handle of her picket sign gripped horizontally like a jouster's lance, the tip itself aimed straight at my heart.

"Good luck," Mandy said and faded into the background.

"Those two are breaking the law," Tiffany shouted over the continuous cry of the horn. "They're just rude. The teachers in the parking lot have the right to leave freely. If those people keep blocking that driveway, I'm not going to stay on this picket line another day."

"They're not breaking the law," I said, seeking to protect my marchers. "It's a public sidewalk—and they are, in fact, letting people leave."

"I don't care," she yelled. "They're radicals. What they're doing goes way beyond picketing. Look what happened at Kent State. I'm sure there are others out here who feel the same way I do." To be certain I got the message, she threw her sign down, then turned abruptly, and marched off in the direction of her car. "Solidarity Forever," her sign read.

"Right," I muttered, scooping up the sign and hurrying over to Jack and Betty. They were busy watching Frick who'd gotten out of his car and retrieved some tools from the back seat. Just then, he was frantically tinkering under the hood.

I had to speak loudly to be heard over the horn. "Tiffany says she'll go back in if you guys keep this up."

"Oh, come on," Jack said equally loud. "This is nothing. People like Tiffany look for anything to complain about. Kids were shot today on an American college campus."

"Protesters block freeways and railroad tracks all the time," Betty said. "This is just a parking lot."

"Come on, Art," Jack railed. "In some schools the striking teachers pour glue into the gate-locks so the scabs can't get out at all. Believe me, tomorrow Tiffany will be back on the line."

I shook my head. "We need harmony out here, Jack," I shouted. "We've been strong for three weeks. Let's not lose—" sudden silence; Frick had shut down the horn "—anybody now," I found myself needlessly hollering.

Okay, I felt silly, but at least I'd gotten my message across. Like a pair of reprimanded children, Jack and Betty slowly nodded their acquiescence.

At the same time, Frick roared out of the parking lot, holding his arm out the driver's window—this time high above the roof of the Pontiac—and once more waving his middle finger.

"Not too original, is he?" said Jack.

The former union rep turned out to be right on two counts. Not only was Don Frick not original, but the next day Tiffany Schwartz returned to the picket line.

🎓

One morning in mid-May as we walked together in front of the school, Mandy said, "Most of the time I can count on my father to help me when I'm in a financial bind."

"I guess you told him you're on strike then," I laughed.

"It's in the news," Mandy said. "Even as far away as New York. You know, my dad's really nice. He paid for my car when I couldn't afford one. But I can assure you that he won't be paying my rent— not if I'm participating in what I'm certain he'd call left-wing activities."

"Believe me, I sympathize. So far, we've all lost close to a month's salary."

"Well," she said, speaking quite slowly now, "I've been giving the subject a lot of thought, and I had this idea. Somebody told me how I might be able to reduce my rent. I could give up my apartment and—"

I stopped walking. Suddenly, I realized what she was trying to tell me, and I grabbed both of her hands.

"Are you sure about this?"

She nodded. "As I said, I've thought a lot about it. Forgive the silly way I've approached the subject because I really do want to take a chance on us. I really do want to be with you."

We stood in the middle of the sidewalk. Fellow picketers had to walk around us and angle their signs away so they wouldn't hit our heads while we talked this out.

"Are you sure?" I asked again.

"As sure as I can be right now. Is anyone ever completely sure about such things?" Her green eyes were open wide as she posed the question.

I couldn't think of anything to say; I just stood there on the picket line squeezing her hands.

"Here's the thing, Art. I really enjoy being with you, and I think the two of us are worth the try."

I didn't need to hear any more. "And you'll work it out with your dad?" I asked.

"I mean, I've told him we're dating. But just like you said, I'll tell him I'm going to get a new place with a roommate—in order to save money— 'cause of the strike. It's the truth, even if it's not exactly the reason."

Then—right there in front of everybody—she threw her arms around me and kissed me hard on the lips.

"I'll tell Dad about my new roommate some other time," she said softly.

🎓

As it turned out, Mandy really had devoted lots of thought to the matter. She surprised me by deciding that she didn't need to hang on to her apartment after all; and eager to move, she gave notice to her landlord that she was leaving and arranged with the post office to forward her mail. If it was okay with me, she hoped to move in to my place during the coming weekend.

"Fantastic," I said.

"I'll need somewhere to put my clothes," she said Saturday morning as she dropped a kaleidoscopic bundle of skirts and blouses onto the vinyl couch in my living room. Clearly, my apartment's tiny closet wasn't large enough. Next to the clothes she tossed her orange velour pillow. She was gentler with her books, sorting them into small stacks on my coffee table. I helped her carry in a few cardboard boxes filled with her teaching materials.

Late that afternoon we drove to a discount furniture store on Robertson and bought a metal stand-up closet.

"Our first joint purchase," I said as we pooled our cash at the checkout register.

Fitting the metal closet into the trunk of the Dart took some doing; but we twisted and turned it in such a way that, although it stuck out over the rear bumper, it seemed secure enough not to fall out. Besides, the drive was only a few blocks.

I parked in front of Mrs. Gross' building, and together Mandy and I carried the closet past the bright-red bougainvillea lining the pathway to the back, past the apple tree, up the metal stairs, and into the apartment. To make room inside the small bedroom, we stacked one of my two bureaus on top of the other and eased the stand-up closet into the newly vacated space.

We brought over the rest of Mandy's stuff on Sunday—her cane lamp, her pens, her ink. We mounted some of her drawings above the bookshelves in the living room, and we moved a few books around to make space for her potted succulents and the pothos. I screwed a new hook into the ceiling above the desk to give the spider-plant a place to hang.

On Monday, Mandy and I drove to school together for the first time.

Chapter Eleven

The Olympic Auditorium

*W*e relished our new arrangement. More personal time together. Less stress. No need to arrange dates or drive two cars to work or do grocery-shopping separately. Now, as the teachers' strike moved into its fourth week, we could worry about our professional lives full-time together. When would our teaching careers return to normal? When might we begin earning salaries again?

Actually, the first indication of a serious end to the strike occurred at the start of the following week. On Monday before school, Janice Storm, the union's field representative for all of the west side, pulled up to our picket line in her white Cadillac. I'd met her a few times at meetings, and I walked around to the driver's side to see what was up.

"Big news," she greeted me through the open window. "Last night, the district agreed to a binding contract." She ran a hand through her short dark hair, then peered up at me over the top of her sunglasses. "They're offering a five-percent raise."

"Not bad," I said. "Sounds like the political pressure—the letters, the phone calls, all that stuff—must have finally swayed them."

"Let's not get ahead of ourselves," Janice cautioned. "We're just getting started here. No matter how long you've been walking the line, you can't claim a strike has even begun until management makes its first offer. It can take days or weeks or even a whole lot longer."

"Still, five percent sounds pretty good. What's the catch?"

She smiled up at me. "You have to return to work."

"Yeah, well," I said.

Janice handed me a flyer. "Here. Read this. It'll tell you all you need to know. Now I gotta go."

I skimmed the printed sheet as she drove off. There was a quick summary of the school district's proposal—the five percent raise and the new contract Janice had just mentioned. Though there was nothing about smaller class sizes and better working conditions, there was also a pledge from the superintendent that any minor problems—like guaranteeing there'd be no recriminations against the striking teachers—would be resolved after we returned to work. The flyer also announced the details of a general membership meeting the next day to debate the board's proposal.

No sooner did my fellow-picketers see me talking with Janice than they figured something important was brewing. It wasn't difficult to gather

154

everyone together in front of Corny's station wagon so I could give them the news.

"On the surface," I told the group, "the deal sounds pretty good. I mean, it promises us a real contract as well as a raise." Channeling Janice's words, I hastened to add, "But don't forget that this is just their first offer. Think of it as recognition of our power. If they've agreed to a five percent raise now, we should be able to pressure them for more."

"Well," Tiffany Schwartz said, "I think we should take them up on what they've already offered. Then we can go back to work."

Some teachers nodded; most looked wary.

"It doesn't seem right to me," Sarah Mertz said softly. "A month of striking, and yet they want us to return to our classrooms without fully explaining the details."

"First, you negotiate," proclaimed Annie Smith, holding up a finger for each of the steps she counted off. "Then you settle, and then you go back to work."

"Like Art said," Jack reminded everyone, "this is just an opening offer. All it really means is that they're afraid of us—we'd be foolish to give in so easily."

"It'd be like punting on first down," said Sam Turner. "And let's not forget smaller classes."

Murmurs of agreement underscored Sam's words. Tiffany's scowl suggested dissent, and she wasn't alone. Lots of people were just plain tired.

"Save your questions and complaints until tomorrow," I said. "The whole point of the big union meeting is to let everybody sound off. No official vote is scheduled yet."

"Where's it going to be?" Sam asked.

"The Olympic Auditorium," I smiled.

To accommodate the thousands of striking teachers, the union had rented the famous sports arena at Eighteenth and Grand, a landmark of Los Angeles culture since the mid-1920s. I remembered going there as a kid with my dad in the '50s to watch wrestlers like Wild Red Berry and Gorgeous George throw their weight around. Back then, everybody knew the phone number: Richmond 9-5171. It was a place where boxers (Thursday nights), wrestlers (Wednesday and Friday nights) and roller-derby skaters (weekends) did their thing.

The news of a possible settlement sparked nervous energy in the strikers. When our group broke up, people started talking among themselves. We all knew the score. The strike had already lasted over a month; and now—for better or for worse—an end might actually be in sight.

The sun shone brightly Tuesday afternoon when Jack and Betty joined Mandy and me in the Dart for the drive downtown. We wanted to arrive early since I'd asked everybody to gather in the parking lot behind the arena an hour before the start of the meeting.

"There'll be lots of speakers critical of prolonging the strike," Janice had warned me on the phone the night before. "They'll argue that we've been out too long. They'll say that any kind of settlement will be better than losing more money."

"And lots of my people will agree," I'd said. "It's just a question of how many."

"I get that, Art," Janice had said. "But you have to convince them that there's more to be gotten. Give your people a final pep talk before you go into the meeting. Tell them to keep the faith. Tell them to be ready for all the negativity the dissenters are sure to create."

Mid-day traffic was light, and it took us less than half-an-hour to get from our picket line at Phillips to the Olympic. Though surrounded by thousands of sign-waving teachers, the aging arena looked just as I'd remembered: a huge pale box with a plain façade, its doors and ticket-windows partially hidden in the shadows of overhanging arches.

I'll be honest. I had anticipated a reflective atmosphere, a contemplative scene in which we'd discuss the fate of education in the second largest school district in the country. But as soon as we entered the parking lot, a super-charged circus exploded that idea.

First, the noise—vendors hawking food from the tables and stalls ringing the lot, foot-long hot dogs sizzling on grills, bells tinkling, and boom boxes dueling.

Then, all the color—electric-blue cotton candy; coiled red licorice; multiple signs for chocolate-and-white Eskimo Pies and red, orange, and purple Popsicles; longhaired hippies pushing gaudy, tie-dyed tee shirts in all the tints of the rainbow.

Not to be left out, of course, the eccentrics: angry radicals waving copies of *The Militant, The Daily Worker,* and *The Berkeley Barb*; fired-up feminists and fist-raising Black-power-advocates handing out newsletters; flower-wielding, end-the-war activists selling "Peace-Now" pins and bumper stickers or dancing to the rock-beats pumped out by the competing stereos.

And framing the entire scene, thousands of teachers marching slowly around the block, their bobbing white signs displaying their battle cries: "An Apple a Day Doesn't Pay the Bills," "Size Does Matter," "Teachers Want What Children Need."

I managed to maneuver the Dart through the madness and into the Olympic's parking lot. It took a while, but I found a space to park, and once we were out of the car, Mandy and I began waving our signs so the other Phillips teachers could see us. Corny Whittaker waved back with her cane; and she, Sam Turner, Marc Whisk, and Harry Barnes pushed their way through the crowd in our direction. Soon, others—Jack and Betty among them—were catching up. Minutes later Tiffany Schwartz joined the group.

"The board's offer is just an opening," I reminded everybody after they'd gathered around me. "It only proves they know we're hanging tough. Think how much more we can gain if we stick it out."

The Phillips teachers cheered and shook their signs in approval.

"Don't cave," I pleaded. "Don't be misled by any crazy claims or charges you hear inside."

People clapped in support.

"Listen to him," Corny urged, raising her cane.

More cheering and sign-waving.

"Power to the people," Jack hollered through cupped hands.

"Right on," Betty shouted.

I raised a fist. "Let's keep it going."

The Phillips teachers raised their fists as well.

"Okay, then," I said, "it's time to get our seats." And together we Phillips strikers marched off towards the arena.

A trio of doorways comprise the main entrance to the Olympic, and it didn't take long to reach the three lines of teachers waiting to enter them. Most of the Phillips people joined the middle queue, and it eventually led us into the dimly-lit lobby.

Inside, we merged with the other two lines to form a tightly-packed human wedge that advanced only a couple of feet before coming to a halt. Stuck in the gloom like that, we remained squeezed together, enveloped in a low rumble of muted voices and the stink of sweating bodies.

Though it seemed much longer, it was only minutes until we began to move again, inching our way across the lobby into an even darker, tunnel-like passage coated in a sour mélange of stale popcorn, peanuts, and cooking oil. At the far end, a dimly lit archway, no doubt the entrance into the auditorium itself, seemed to offer relief. Shuffling towards the glow, we could hear the din of voices growing louder. And yet, no sooner did we reach the arch than we saw people already inside shaking their heads.

"No room!" they shouted. "Go up!"

Once more the mass pushed on, this time in the direction of a darkened stairwell a few feet further along. Slowly, we edged forward and, upon reaching the staircase, began the cramped, tedious climb to the next level. When we finally got to the archway at the top, we could breathe a little easier. The crowding lessened, and we passed into the arena proper.

Eyes closed, the smell of cigar smoke and stale beer could tell you where you were. But that was nothing compared to the overpowering roar that engulfed us. It took a few moments to distinguish— two mighty choruses challenging each other, the fate of the school board's offer hanging in the balance. From one camp, chants of "no"; from the other, cheers of "yes," along with spirited clapping and heavy stomping that shook the building.

Amidst the chaos, we secured a number of empty seats, and the Phillips teachers settled in as a group. The Olympic can hold some ten thousand fans; and as more and more people filed in, the cavernous hall rocked all the louder.

Mandy and I, seated in the middle of our group, added our voices to the crescendo of "No's" swelling ever louder. We wanted the whole world to hear that the striking teachers from Phillips Junior High School weren't about to be bought off by some eleventh-hour agreement. Hell no! Not by some feeble offer mainly designed to get us to go back to work. Even Tiffany Schwartz stood bobbing and weaving in time to the cries of protest erupting from our section.

Through the haze of cigarette smoke now clouding the air, you could see the arena floor far below us. It was illuminated by the old metal truss used to light up the boxing ring and framed by the L.A. Thunderbirds' black Roller-derby track. At the center of the steeply-banked oval, a row of red folding chairs and a makeshift podium complete with table and microphone had been set up. A section of the straightaway had been removed, so people could walk to the infield without having to negotiate the slope of the track. While some union people down there were still milling about, others had already taken their seats, including a couple of cigar-smoking heavyweights in fedoras.

A moment later, I pointed out the sandy-haired figure dressed in brown who was seating himself between the two large smokers. "Neil James," I said, "the union president."

"Who are those guys on each side of him?" Mandy asked. "They look like extras from a gangster movie."

I laughed. "Janice said some union big-shots from the East Coast would be here."

Janice herself was seated in the infield next to Sam Woods, the crusty, eighty-year-old lawyer who served as the union's director of legal affairs. Sam was the "go-to" guy for teachers who encountered any legal problems with the school board. I also recognized the union's executive director, Mel Avrutin. Even as high up as we were sitting, I could see the stylish dark blazer and contrasting khaki slacks that marked him as one of the union's PR men.

Some ten minutes passed before various officials down on the floor raised their hands to quiet the crowd, and only after another ten did the volume begin to wane. The odd random cheer still erupted— "Reject the offer!" "Seal the deal!"—and an energetic murmur continued to hum, but Neil James finally strode to the microphone and raised his fist.

"Power to the people!" he shouted. "Power to the teachers."

A new explosion of acclamation.

"Solidarity forever."

More whooping and sign waving. It took an additional five minutes for the auditorium to calm down.

When it did, James was ready. Pointing his finger back and forth as he spoke, the way President Kennedy used to, he declared, "We go back on our own terms, or we don't go back at all."

Another frenzy of shouting, clapping, stomping.

Once more the union president waited for silence. When it arrived, he began to highlight aspects of the board's proposal—the binding contract and the five-percent raise in particular. Voting on the offer would take place at the end of the week. A yes-vote would signify acceptance and an end to the strike; a no-vote would prolong our struggle until a more acceptable conclusion could be reached.

A number of speakers followed, union officials advocating one position or the other, but each in agreement that all of us had to make up our own minds and accept the group's decision.

"This is a democratic union," Neil James proclaimed when the speakers had concluded, "and we all know that teachers are great believers in democracy."

"As an ideal anyway," I whispered to Mandy.

"No," she said, "in reality. A democratic vote will decide our fate."

She was right, of course—however unpopular the decision might be.

Just then someone handed Neil James a note. He read it, turned to look off into the darkness behind him, and after a moment faced his audience again.

"It has come to my attention," the union president announced, his voice echoing throughout the arena, "that we have two additional speakers who've only just now arrived. All of you should understand that they were not invited, and yet they are requesting permission to address you. In the name of academic freedom, I suggest that we listen to what they have to say."

James paused, and you could hear the word "who?" skipping back and forth among the crowd.

"Both speakers," he said, "are members of the school board."

Howls of protest greeted the news.

He nodded in sympathy and yet at the same time raised his hands to quell the churning hostility. "Let us not forget that the two members in question are also our only friends downtown."

James was obviously referring to the two liberals on the seven-man school board—Juan Torres, a medical doctor (the same board member to whom Jack wanted to send the evaluation forms), and the ironically named Alfred Teacher, a professor of public speaking, at L.A. State. Nonetheless, resistance tore through the crowd.

A shout of "No management stooges" wafted above the other whines and chants. A torrent of irate stomping and angry catcalls followed, drowning out the president even as he tried to regain some order.

Suddenly, as if an angel had delivered the message from on-high, a fresh cry penetrated the din. "Freedom of Speech" it demanded, and all around us people absorbed the sentiment.

"We're a democracy," someone else cried out, and the repetitive chant of "Free Speech, Free Speech" broke loose.

"They're our guests," Tiffany Schwartz said to no one in particular. "In the name of fairness, we should hear what they have to say."

Fairness, I thought. There's that word again.

Jack, who was sitting behind us, bent forward. "Who's to say that one man's fairness is not another man's deceit?" he asked. "You've got to wonder if these impromptu speeches were planned in advance."

"Neil James only just got that note," I reminded him.

Jack grinned. He preferred his conspiracy theory. "What if James thinks he can't maintain the strike any longer? Or what if the board has offered him a sweet deal to end things quickly? What better way of convincing us to go back in than by letting outsiders do the dirty work? That way, he stays clean. If Torres and Teacher are the ones who get us to call off the strike, it won't be Neil James's fault."

"At least, it won't look like it was," I said. That was the moment it first dawned on me. Although the money-offer sounded good, our noble struggle for smaller classes and a fair contract could end in a gigantic sell-out—buy the teachers off and forget the rest.

Our eyes wide open now, Mandy and I leaned forward for a better view of the political drama unfolding on the stage below.

Dr. Torres was first. A short, dark, bearded man in a navy-blue suit, he strode boldly to the microphone.

Sarcastic cries of "¡Viva la Huelga!" and "¡Viva la Causa!" rang through the arena.

His message was simple and unequivocal. With the hint of a Spanish accent, he proclaimed, "You must end your strike, my friends!"

"No!" People shouted back. "Never!"

Torres shook his head. "Accept the contract offer, my friends; we can get you no better deal. Of that I am certain."

"Try harder," somebody yelled.

"We do our best," Torres said. He followed those words with a departing salute and quickly exited the scene.

Hoots and boos accompanied the man's hurried walk from the podium. And yet if I perceived the mood correctly, his rude and loud-mouthed critics seemed to be generating in their fellow teachers a sense of antagonism towards the hecklers. Mandy grabbed my hand as the first speaker rushed off, and I sensed that she shared the same impression I did.

Dr. Torres' quick retreat left the microphone open for the tall and gangly Alfred Teacher, and you couldn't help noticing how slowly he came forward. It was as if the new speaker was consciously allowing the emerging hostility towards those who belittled his school-board colleague to have time to transform into full-blown sympathy for himself. For all I knew, such had been the plan of the two speakers from the start.

As the speech professor stood before us, his shaved head reflecting the bright lights from the truss, you could feel a growing appreciation in the crowd for a man unafraid to face so hostile an audience. Then again, Alfred Teacher was a master of public speaking, a master of understanding full well how to exploit an audience's vulnerability.

The professor rested his long arms on the podium—the teacher waiting for a noisy classroom to settle down. When it did, he dived right in—no greeting, no salutation, just immediate identification with our problems.

"I'm sick—" he began, but he'd barely gotten the words out before a barrage of mock-sympathetic groans greeted him.

"I'm tired," he lamented, and another chorus of derisive cries swelled up.

But the professor would not be derailed. He began again, more quickly this time in order to complete his thought. "I am sick and tired of being on the short end of every vote we take whenever Dr. Torres and I try to support you."

His blatant allegiance to our cause took many in the arena by surprise, and more than a few people started listening more closely. It was as if his defense of our struggle was stoking the audience's remorse for their attack on Torres, a union "friend" who, like the professor himself, was on our side.

To me, it seemed a clear effort by Teacher to manipulate the strikers, an obvious attempt to convert the crowd's initial hostility into collective guilt, not only for having insulted Torres, but also for the much grander—and unspoken—transgression of shutting down the schools, of depriving innocent children of their education.

"You simply don't have the votes on the school board," Teacher continued, his audience listening ever more intently. "Five-to-two-against on every ballot will not get you what you want. You're better off taking what the board offers you now because, believe me, those Philistines at the Fort are not going to give you anything better."

It didn't take much to discern the professor's game-plan. By insulting his conservative district colleagues, he was effectively severing both Torres and himself from the rest of the school board. Here was an ally, people were thinking—or wanted to think—or needed to think—somebody in a position to know what was really going on, somebody on our side who was telling us that prolonging the strike was useless. The silence in the hall suggested the professor had scored some points.

Teacher paused a few beats after delivering his "carrot." He clearly wanted more time before daring to present the "stick"—although by separating himself and Torres from the rest of the board, he'd already spoken as if the two of them weren't part of the assemblage of tyrants wielding it. "The board majority wants to call in the police," he announced at last. "I'm telling you—"

Jack leaned in again. "Warning's more like it."

"—the reactionaries on the board want to send paddy wagons out to every school in the district and round up the picketing teachers. Paddy wagons! Do you understand what I'm saying? Those fascists at the Fort want to arrest you people if you don't go back to work. They want to put you in jail."

He paused again to allow the implications to sink in.

Mandy dropped my hand. "They wouldn't dare," she said, defiance in her eyes. "They don't have the nerve."

Mandy could put things into perspective, draw a conclusion, and never look back. I, on the other hand, wasn't so sure. Maybe the others on the board really did want to arrest us. Maybe Teacher and Torres actually were our friends. At the very least, Teacher had raised the stakes. According to the professor, we were all being threatened with jail— dedicated citizens facing arrest—the Free Speech Movement all over again. I hadn't been ready to take such a stand back in Berkeley. Now I was seeing things differently.

By leading the Phillips teachers out on strike, I'd made my commitment—I'd already told Mandy as much. Not only was I risking my career, but also (as Mandy had been quick to remind me) my draft deferment. Without a teaching job, I could end up in Vietnam. Yet this time around, I was determined not to let the school district scare me. Students at Cal had been arrested for defending free speech. People were going to prison for refusing the draft. Why, students at Kent State had been killed by the National Guard. I was finally angry enough to play the odds.

"You teachers have proved your point," the professor proclaimed. "Job well done. But my advice now? Accept the board's offer and return to work. It's your only chance for success." He raised a fist in solidarity and, striding away from the podium, disappeared somewhere into the darkness, a mixture of catcalls and applause accompanying his exit.

It required but a brief look around the arena to see that attitudes had changed. Apparently, lots of my colleagues were reaching a conclusion not only different from my own but also different from the one they themselves had come in with. As Mandy and I sat there in the long, drawn-out silence, it was as if I could hear the crumbling of the union's collective will.

Torres and Teacher had fulfilled their assignment most effectively—our so-called "uninvited" speakers had snuffed out the spirit of rebellion. At that moment, I didn't think there was anyone left in the Olympic who could convince the majority of teachers there to reject the board's opening offer. Our two so-called "friends" on the board may have truly supported the striking teachers; but they were also representatives of the school district, and their immediate responsibility was to get us to go back to work.

"We're done," I said to Mandy, my tone grim.

When it was time for members of the rank-and-file to have their say, plenty of people lined up at the two open mics down on the arena floor, and some did cry out for extending the strike. Dying gasps. The wild pro-strike enthusiasm that had filled the Olympic upon our arrival had evaporated—or been co-opted. The individuals who dared to argue for prolonging the walkout received only a smattering of applause.

Then things got even worse. A reading teacher commandeered one of the microphones and announced in a high-pitched voice: "First, we end the strike. Then we show our good faith. Let's convince the public that our actions have been honorable. Let's agree to donate our five-percent raise to the district's reading program."

Ordinarily, teachers would have howled down the ridiculous notion of giving back to the school board a penny of their pay, let alone a five-percent raise. But the opposition was spent. A few boos erupted only to be drowned out by an overwhelming wave of cheers. Signs bobbed up and down and swayed right and left. As far as I was concerned, reason had left the building.

Far below us, Neil James was huddling with the two burly men I assumed were union executives from the East Coast. He placed a hand on each of their broad shoulders. They conversed a while longer; and then, after exchanging nods and slaps on the back, James returned to the microphone.

"I pledge," he proclaimed loudly, his voice booming around the arena, "to put this pay-issue on the ballot. It'll be right there alongside the decision to accept or reject the board's offer." Then, amid a whirlwind of exhortations from the crowd, he shouted into the mic: "I hereby declare this meeting adjourned."

A new clamor now arose as chants of "Yes" from more and more teachers filled the air. Not only was the roar louder than the cries that had greeted us at the start, but this time the tension was missing. There was little opposition.

"It's one thing to read about mob psychology," I said to Mandy. "It's something else again when you know the individuals in the mob."

"Let's get out of here," she said, taking my arm.

Turning to go, we couldn't miss seeing Tiffany Schwartz waving a yellow pencil like a baton. She was leading her Phillips colleagues in a disheartening chorus of affirmation.

Chapter Twelve

The Vote

*G*ive them credit; the union worked quickly. Just hours after the meeting at the Olympic, the telephone tree carried the message that balloting would take place two days later. Voting booths would open for the day at 11:00, Thursday morning, near the carousel in Griffith Park, the rustic sprawl of rolling hills, twisting brooks, and wooded glens that lies just north of downtown.

Mandy's and my votes were no mystery: The board's initial offer revealed to everyone that the district was ready to compromise. To us, prolonging the strike made total sense: such a strategy offered a better chance of benefitting the lives of teachers than prematurely concluding the walkout did. Yet most of our colleagues—originally opposed to settling— had changed their minds. Not Jack, of course, or Betty or a few others.

I clung to hope. Maybe that rush to end matters had simply been the product of all the emotion at the Olympic. Maybe once outside that frenzied cauldron, people might be willing to rethink their positions. Figuring I should try one last time to get them to reconsider, I activated the Phillips telephone tree the night before the vote and recommended a ten o'clock meeting the next morning at the picnic grounds near the Griffith Park carousel.

🎓

Beneath a morning sky still washed in gray, the sweet scent of wet grass filled the air. Surrounded by a scattering of sycamores and oaks, Mandy and I stood waiting by the old wooden tables near the carousel for the Phillips teachers to arrive. The merry-go-round itself was closed—the band-organ silent and the seventy or so carved prancing horses frozen in the shadows of the red-and-white roof.

Soon, random groups of district teachers came crunching their way down sloping gravel paths from the parking lots atop a nearby hill. The newcomers fanned out to various locations, some to picnic areas not far from us, others to spots beneath distant trees. Clearly, we weren't the only school conducting pre-vote discussions that morning.

As the Phillips teachers gravitated towards our meeting place, they displayed none of the boisterous camaraderie we had cultivated on the picket line, and today Corny had brought no bagels. Exchanging only the most subdued handshakes or polite nods, people took seats on the weathered benches or found places behind them to stand.

"Good luck," Mandy said as I stepped forward and stared out at the collection of tired faces.

"I'm not going to repeat all the arguments you've already heard about rejecting the board's offer," I announced to the group.

Jack, who could read the downcast looks as well as anyone, rewarded me with three slow, sarcastic handclaps.

"But I do want to make one final point about the salary give-away."

"Just ridiculous," somebody muttered.

"That five percent is our money," I said, "Let's not vote to give it to a reading program that should be paid for by the public."

"Right on," somebody else shouted.

"Oh, come now," said Tiffany Schwartz, the impatience in her voice telling me to get on with it, "donating our money to reading makes us look good."

She wasn't alone in her opinion. The strike had taken its toll. From all the detached expressions and folded arms before me, I figured that at the same time I was being politely listened to, I was also being politely ignored. Bottom line—people wanted the whole thing over with.

"Remember," I said, trying to put off the impending doom, "the proposal we're voting on today is just the board's opening offer. They expected us to reject it as soon as they thought it up. If we stick together and vote 'no' as a bloc—and the other schools do the same—we can still get more. Don't forget our call for smaller classes."

No sooner had I concluded my little speech and people began preparing to head for the polling booths than Mandy suddenly got to her feet and turned to address the crowd. "Wait," she said. It was the first time she'd spoken publicly during the strike, and most all of her colleagues paused to listen. "You know what I've learned during my first year of teaching?"

"What?" somebody shouted.

"Tell us, Mandy," Sam Turner said.

"That teachers who want to be treated professionally and don't do anything to make it happen get what they deserve—nothing."

"We don't get anything anyway," Tiffany said. "The public isn't behind us, and without public opinion on our side we have no strength."

"Public opinion be damned," red-faced Union Jack shouted. He ran his hand across his bald head. "We know there's more to this job than standing in front of a bunch of kids and talking. But that's all that most people think we do, and those are the very people who think they can tell us how to teach."

Agreement percolated through the crowd.

"You know what?" Jack railed. "If the public really were on our side, I'd start thinking we were doing something wrong."

I applauded Jack's words, and Mandy joined me. So did Corny Whittaker. And Betty Warden.

And the new teacher, Harry Barnes. And a few others. But the applause didn't mean they were all supporting Jack's position. When people finally did get up to leave, their grim looks told me the strike was over.

Jack took Mandy's hand. "You delivered timely words," he told her and kissed her on the cheek. After which, he walked over to Corny and kissed her cheek as well. In the process, he slipped a fifty-dollar bill into her palm. "To help pay for the bagels," he whispered.

Then we all went to vote.

The district announced the results three days later. By a four-to-one margin across the city, the union's teachers had accepted the school board's offer. They also voted to subsidize the reading program with our salary raise.

The Los Angeles Teachers' Strike of 1970 was history.

Ironically, within a week after the votes had been counted, the superintendent undercut the union's good faith. The strikers didn't represent all of the teachers in the district, he said, and therefore he couldn't accept the union's "generous offer" to donate our raise to the district's reading-program.

"On strike four-and-a-half weeks," Jack smirked, "and we couldn't even vote to give away our money."

Jeremy Goodman put it another way: "Teachers suck shit through straws."

🎓

We returned to work on the Monday after the vote-count was announced. Though I imagine that most of us took some pleasure in staring down the teachers who had crossed our picket lines, it didn't take long for people on opposite sides of the strike to resume the same relationships they'd maintained before the walkout.

As far as I could tell, the strike produced only two new meaningful developments within the Phillips faculty, and neither had anything to do with politics. Corny Whittaker came back to work, and Mandy and I now left for school in the same car from the same address.

I wasn't the only one to note that last development, however. On the morning we returned to our classrooms, Vivian Laws stood just outside the red double-doors at the school's entrance. Since it was a position he often assumed in order to monitor the arriving students, I wasn't particularly surprised to see him there.

Yet on this occasion he wasn't watching the kids. In his familiar stance—arms folded, legs spread—he was staring in the direction of the faculty parking lot. More precisely, he was watching Mandy and me walk up the sidewalk together, turn onto the pathway leading to the main building, and approach the red double-doors at the school's entrance, the entrance which I'm sure that in his paternalistic mind he viewed himself as guarding.

Chapter Thirteen

Storm Clouds

*I*n the middle of our second week back from the strike, Betty Warden yanked open the door to my classroom. The school day had ended and the kids were gone, but she didn't have her usual smile as she motioned me to follow.

"What going on?" I asked when I realized she was leading me next door.

Then I saw Mandy. She was sitting at a student's desk near the front of Betty's empty room, and she was weeping.

For a moment I stood motionless; then I raced to her side. "What's the matter?" I asked, but it was clear she was in no condition to speak. Holding her tight, I looked over her shoulder at Betty.

"Laws observed her period five," Betty said. "Right after, he gave her the 'come-into-my office' bit. He had some unkind things to say, and—" Betty gestured at the distraught Mandy — "you can see the result. It was her free period, but you still had a class. Since it was my free period too, she came in here."

I was shocked. Until that moment, I thought I had a pretty good understanding of Vivian Laws and his hard-nosed attitude. Sure, in her first evaluation he'd complained about Mandy's teaching, but I figured such criticizing is what lots of administrators do to new teachers—establishing who's the boss, so to speak.

New teacher that she was, Mandy had taken Laws at his word. In December, he'd asked for more creativity in her history classes, so during the second semester she tried a number of fresh approaches. She used maps and plans devised by students to show how small towns evolved into large cities. She took her kids on field trips to the county art museum to see paintings that illustrated American history. She even ran two old-time, small-gauge electric trains in her classroom to dramatize how the West had been populated. With the school year almost over, there was no reason to believe that Mandy's teaching had been anything but excellent.

"At least, I didn't cry in his office," she said, catching her breath as she spoke. "He said that my classroom was boring. He told me I was boring."

"Oh, come on," I said, shaking my head. "He'd never put such bullshit in writing."

Betty handed Mandy a tissue.

"In how many different ways," I said to nobody in particular, "can they tell us they don't think what we do is important?"

Mandy received her written evaluation the next day. If a penalty hadn't gone with it, you might have called Laws's criticism a joke—both contradictory and topsy-turvy. At the end of the first semester, he'd instructed Mandy to teach more creatively; this time around—after the model trains and the map work and the field trips—he told her that she should rely more on basics.

"I'll bet he doesn't even remember what he wrote in the first evaluation," I said. "You know how he is—he probably just wanted to say something critical to make sure you remember who's in charge."

"Yes, but—" Mandy countered, her unfinished sentence floating off somewhere.

I had minimized Laws's comments at the end of the fall semester; this time, however, I knew Mandy should be concerned. Not that Laws's written words caused a problem. He'd cited "poor planning" as the basis for his criticism even though such a complaint could be completely repudiated by the praise Mandy had gotten from Sam Turner. To be sure, a department chair's comments are merely advisory, but during the first half of the school year Laws himself had considered Mandy's planning satisfactory.

No, the damning part of the principal's review appeared in the little box at the bottom of the page, the summary section where Laws had rendered judgment on the entirety of Mandy's first year of teaching.

He had one of three choices. He should have checked "meets or exceeds standard performance" as he'd done the previous semester. He could even have—wrongly—marked "unsatisfactory," which Mandy's teaching clearly was not. Instead, he'd settled for "below standard performance," a nebulous assessment somewhere in the gray area between the other two. It was a gutless call. Until then, it never occurred to me that crushing a new teacher could be the man's actual intent. Such a goal, I would have thought, was too low even for Vivian Laws.

"I want the union," Mandy said, her face flushed with anger. "Vivian Laws is not going to ruin my career." She slapped her hand down hard on the evaluation form and stared at me, her eyes at their most penetrating green. "You're my rep. Call the union."

Mandy and I sat on the vinyl couch in our living room waiting for a return-call from Janice Storm, the union's field rep. Though neither one of us could think about much else, we still attempted to grade students' essays. Soon enough we discovered that the loops and swirls of their writing failed to engage.

Just before six, a shrill ring interrupted the silence. "Finally," I said, going over to the desk and picking up the phone.

"After school tomorrow we'll set him straight," Janice said after I'd filled her in on Mandy's plight. "We're going to beat him on this. He can't go around insulting teachers and then ding them on their evaluation and expect to get away with it."

"Meeting tomorrow," I mouthed to Mandy.

Seemingly mollified by the idea, she nodded agreement. Yet in the middle of the night, I was awakened by a harsh grating sound: Mandy grinding her teeth as she slept.

We met Janice Storm after school the next day in front of the principal's office. Reassuringly professional in black tie and white-linen business suit, the union's west-side rep escorted Mandy into Laws's inner sanctum. I caught a glimpse of the closed blinds and yellow lamp inside the office just before Laws shut the door. Fortunately, this battle would be fought by a union professional, not by a mere union volunteer like me. All I had to do was sit around and wait.

The clock behind Annette Avalon's desk ticked off a minute or two, and once again I found myself staring at the portrait of David Graham Phillips on the office wall. Despite his stolid look of conviction, he offered no assurances, and so, with little insight to be gained from staring at his picture— let alone encountering anyone I might actually have to talk with—I trudged back to my classroom. There were always papers to grade.

Fifteen minutes later the two women came up to get me. From Mandy's blank expression, I couldn't tell what had happened in Laws's office. What I did know was that in order to avoid being overheard, we needed to leave the building before talking.

The three of us headed in the direction of Janice's Cadillac parked in front of the school. I kept looking at Mandy, trying to read from her face what was going on. Had she lost her job? Had Laws caved? But her features remained noncommittal.

When we reached Janice's car, I finally blurted out, "So, how'd it go?"

"No problem," Janice said with a quick smile. "But Amanda can tell you herself."

Mandy shrugged. "I guess Janice is right."

"You guess?"

"Well, we went into Laws's office. That science teacher—"

"Nelly Knopf," I said, "the one who wants to be an administrator."

"But she's so young," Mandy said. "I mean, she's not much older than me."

I just shrugged.

"Anyway, she was already in there as his witness."

Janice looked down to check her watch, a small, diamond-framed circle affixed to a short, white ribbon pinned on her lapel next to her black tie.

The watch hung upside down so she could lift its face upward and read it. "I still have another appointment to get to."

I tried again. "So, what happened?"

Janice gestured in Mandy's direction, as if to say, "You tell him."

"Well," Mandy said, "Mr. Laws read off his list of complaints and claimed they supported the evaluation he gave me."

"What about the things Sam Turner had to say?"

"Nothing."

"What about your classroom being 'boring'?"

"Not to worry," Janice interceded. "I told him he can't go around making vague comments about what does or doesn't appeal to him."

"Oh, I feel better now," I said, my words coated with sarcasm.

"Listen," Janice said, "I stuck up for Amanda. I told your principal that we'd already heard his complaints. I told him that now I wanted to hear some good things."

"And?"

"And he said that he didn't like to list good things about untenured teachers because if he ever wanted to get rid of them, such praise could come back to bite him."

"He actually said that? To you?"

"Yep," Janice said. "Publicly. So, I told him I was going to call the superintendent to see if such

186

double-dealing was school-board policy. I just might—but mainly I raised the issue to make him nervous."

"Cool," I said, feeling a little better, "the superintendent. Maybe somebody besides teachers can get on Laws's case for a change." Then I turned to Mandy. "But what about the evaluation, the 'below-standard-performance' part?"

"Well, Janice said it really isn't anything to worry about."

I wheeled around to face the woman. "What does that mean? I thought that anything below 'meets-or-exceeds' would cost a first-year teacher a probationary contract."

"I beg to differ," she said. "According to the contract we won in the strike, only an 'unsat' can cost you your position. Amanda will automatically receive a second-year contract when this school year ends."

I shook my head in exasperation.

"For whatever it's worth, Art," Mandy shrugged, "Mr. Laws agrees with what you just said—that it has to be 'meets-or-exceeds' to qualify."

I glowered at Janice. She'd been in there with Mandy. She'd heard what Laws had to say, and yet she still didn't think the evaluation was anything to worry about.

Janice put up her hands to calm us. "You know what, Art? You're right. Amanda's evaluation isn't what you want it to be. But it's just one review. Don't you see? As of today, Laws knows that we're going to be on his case all the time. I really don't think she'll be facing any more trouble from him."

"You 'really don't think'?" I said loudly. "And that's it? Hasn't the damage already been done?"

"Wait a minute," Mandy exclaimed, folding her arms. "Don't I get a chance to say something?"

Janice and I turned to Mandy. I think we both were eager to sidestep the tension building between us.

"Look," Mandy said, her words coming quickly, "I don't want to let Mr. Laws get away with any part of this. I want to do something, like reply or respond."

"Good idea," I said. "What do you want to say?"

Mandy's eyes widened, showing off the green. "I want to brag," she proclaimed. "I want to tell how kids enjoy my classes—how my drawings, my maps, my electric trains make history come alive. And I want to include the compliments I got from my department chair. All of that ought to do something to counteract Mr. Laws's evaluation."

"Probably," said Janice with a shrug, "though adding that stuff really isn't necessary."

Stuff? I turned to look at the field rep again. When I had called her, I was hoping for a savior. Now all I could see was a bureaucratic hack. Her responsibility was to help Mandy, and as far as I could tell, she wasn't doing a very good job of it. "Are you sure there's nothing else she needs to do?"

"Relax, will you?" Janice said. "I keep telling you there's nothing to worry about."

"What about how Laws called her 'boring'?"

"I already told you, Art. I warned him about that. Christ, you really are involved in all this, aren't you?"

"I care about her, Janice. I don't want to see her hurt."

Janice's blue eyes lit up. "Ah, finally, I'm beginning to understand." She looked at Mandy whose cheeks, thanks to my choice words, had turned almost as red as her hair.

My heart was pounding, and I took some deep breaths to calm myself. "All I want to know," I said slowly, hands in front of me, palms down, "is that you're sure everything will be all right."

Janice nodded and checked her watch again.

"And next year?" I asked. "What did you say to Laws when he threatened Mandy about her second-year contract?"

"Not to worry," Janice said again, this time with a smile. "I told him what I just told you—that he'd better go back and re-read the rules. The language clearly indicates that a teacher can only be denied a contract with an unsatisfactory evaluation. I assure you that next year Amanda will get the new contract she's entitled to."

All Mandy and I could do was hope Janice was right.

"Now," Janice said, consulting her watch a third time, "I really do have to get going."

Sliding into her Cadillac, she slammed the door shut and waved to Mandy. "Ciao, Amanda," she called and drove off down the street.

Later that evening, Mandy sat at the desk beneath the hanging spider plant and composed a two-page rebuttal that highlighted the strengths of her first year of teaching. The next day, she would send it to district headquarters where, I suspect, it would be placed in her personnel file alongside the principal's evaluation and left to molder in one of the board's cavernous record rooms.

Not soon enough for Mandy and me, the school year ended. We had three months of vacation to enjoy. It seemed far easier to put our faith in Janice Storm and the union than to spend our summer break worrying about the pettiness of Vivian Laws.

Year Two

(September 1970 – June 1971)

Chapter Fourteen

More of the Same

Looking back on that September, we should have begun worrying the week before the semester started. That was when I received the standard letter reminding the Phillips teachers to report to the library for the initial faculty meeting of the school year. Mandy didn't get one, and we both assumed that the post office had simply lost it or that maybe it had never been forwarded from her old address.

We had spent the previous few weeks up north touring the Bay Area. Mandy had never been to San Francisco, and the cable cars and restaurants didn't disappoint. We finished up in Berkeley, and I showed her Sproul Hall where the students were arrested during the Free Speech Movement. More attractive to her architectural eye, however, was the Campanile, Cal's iconic bell tower.

Though Mandy had never been to Europe, she pointed out the tower's similarity to the famous Campanile di San Marco in Venice. I knew that the Berkeley structure was officially named Sather Tower after its donor, but it took Mandy to inform me where its Italian name originated.

Our trip to the campus coincided with a summer session devoid of militant students. As a result, the university's notable activism failed to materialize when a resolution from Senators McGovern and Hatfield to withdraw all American troops from Vietnam was voted down in D.C. During the regular academic year, such a political setback would have roused up the anti-war student body, but it was summer break, and the school remained calm.

When we returned to L.A., I retrieved all the mail Mrs. Gross had kept for us and dumped it onto the desk beneath the hanging spider plant. The slick clothing catalogues and shiny real estate ads were easy to toss; but a pair of return-addresses sparked feelings of dread in both of us that sweltering afternoon the instant we saw them.

The brown envelope with my name on the front came from the Selective Service. Although never welcome, its September arrival was not unexpected. With the national draft-lottery still off in the future, my military status was reassessed at the start of each school year. During the past four, teaching had kept me out of harm's way; but however benevolent my draft board at Santa Monica and Western might have been in protecting students and teachers during previous years, you could never be sure . . . .

I took a deep breath and, slipping my index finger under the flap of the envelope, slowly broke the seal. Inside lay the white card containing the information I was hoping for: II-A, occupational deferment. I'd lucked out again. I still felt bad that some poor soul was out there taking my place, but as long as the system continued to provide me with an out, I would continue to take advantage. I could exhale again.

The other worrisome piece of mail, a pink postal notice for Mandy, informed her that our neighborhood post office was holding a registered letter for her from the school district. Janice Storm's assurances notwithstanding, Mandy's history with Laws prompted concern in both of us.

In fact, Mandy waited till the following afternoon to muster the courage to find out whatever the district had to tell her. "If the news was good," she asked as I drove her to pick up the letter, "why did they have to send it registered?"

"Standard operating procedures," I said, hoping I sounded more positive than I felt.

It took only minutes for Mandy to hustle in and out of the post office. Rushing back to the car with a long white envelope in her hand, she waited till she was seated before opening it and extracting an official-looking sheet of paper. At the top was the district's logo—a small circle containing two crossed wood-pencils below a tiny sun. The sun was emitting rays like lightning bolts into the cleft between the two erasers, just above the point where the pencils crossed. Slowly, she unfolded the page and began to read.

"Oh my God," she screamed.

And then—just like that—there was nothing more to worry about. Janice had been right. According to the letter, the school district had granted Mandy a second-year probationary contract and was returning her to Phillips.

"I don't want to give them the chance to change their minds," she told me; and as soon as we arrived home, she drove downtown to the Fort to sign the contract. Two hours later she returned, waving a copy at me as evidence of her success.

Later that evening the temperature cooled, and we celebrated at The Fox and Hounds. With the school year about to begin, the dinner offered a last chance to enjoy our vacation.

As it turned out, we weren't the only teachers with such a thought. No sooner did we walk into the darkened restaurant than we saw that Tiffany Schwartz had the same idea. Seated alone at a table illuminated by candlelight, she was elegantly attired in a white, off-the-shoulder dress, which nicely complemented her extra-shiny silver hair. In front of her, a full-course meal—salad, vegetables, and some sort of chicken—had been laid out. A crystal flute of bubbling champagne and a half-empty bottle stood just beyond her plate.

Tiffany raised her glass high when she saw us. "To another school year," she said. "To another cruel September."

The sluggish brown haze that blanketed Los Angeles towards the end of one more hot summer made the prospect of going back to work all the less inviting. Worse, once we arrived at school on the pupil-free day, I realized how naïve we'd been.

No sooner did we greet Annette Avalon at the counter in the main office than Vivian Laws appeared before us. Dressed in a black suit, white shirt, and black string tie, he reminded me of a frontier undertaker. Perhaps he had such a role in mind when he motioned Mandy into his office. So smoothly did he manage the scene that I didn't even think of demanding to sit in as her union rep.

Yet as I watched the principal's dark, round form eclipse Mandy as the door closed on the two of them, all that optimism, any good feeling that starting a new year is supposed to signify, evaporated. Our good times up north, her new contract, the sweet taste of sherry at The Fox and Hounds—everything fell away. My insides tightened as I feared what was about to happen in the principal's office.

"Hi, Art," came the jarringly perky voice of Tiffany Schwartz. "Welcome back. It was nice to see you at dinner the other night." Her hair—silver only a few evenings before—was now colored jet black. I could tell from how she stood there fluffing her locks, penciled eyebrows raised, that she expected some sort of excited response from me.

Yet it was all I could do to muster a weak smile, for at that moment the door to Laws's office opened, and Mandy strode out. Though whatever they'd discussed hadn't taken very long, from Mandy's fixed glare and tightly sealed lips, I could tell that she was holding in upsetting news. I extricated myself from Tiffany and followed after Mandy until we reached the relative privacy of the hallway.

"He doesn't want me here," she said simply.

"But the contract—"

She spoke slowly, as if the issue had already been settled, as if she'd already accepted the outcome. "He said the contract doesn't designate schools, and I should never have been reassigned here. The letter that told me to come back to Phillips was wrong."

"Wrong?" I couldn't believe what I was hearing.

"He told me to go downtown and get a new school." There was no sadness in her tone—just resignation. "And that's exactly what I'm going to do, Art. I don't want to work for someone who has no use for me."

I saw little point in arguing. What was there to say—"Stay here and battle the asshole everyday of your career"? Yet I did try to make her feel better. "You know this is just 'cause you had the nerve to cross him."

"Right," she said sharply. "And look where it got me. You can talk; you have tenure. I'm just a lowly second-year teacher, and I'm tired of fighting the man. I don't want to go through another semester like the one I had here last year."

I hated to see her give in. Her tenacity, her strength—that's what makes her unique. Yet I also realized she was right. It didn't matter that she was a great teacher. If she stayed at Phillips, she'd be hassling with Vivian Laws all the time, and going to war against your principal is no way to remain effective in the classroom.

"Take the car downtown and work all this out," I said, swallowing hard. "I'll get a ride home with somebody."

🎓

Vivian Laws plugged in the sound system behind the main desk of the library. A loud pop exploded from the speaker, the final punctuation mark ending summer break. Much of what he said that morning drifted in and out of my consciousness. I heard something about eliminating the "negativism" created by last year's strike and then a few nonsensical words about pumping new energy into the "good ship Phillips."

"Good ship Phillips?" For Mandy, it had been anything but.

Needless to say, her plight didn't bother Laws as he went on to tout "two new accomplishments that everyone can feel proud of." Turning to Penelope Martinez, he asked her to stand. In typical fashion, she rose reluctantly and then immediately sat down.

Quiet and thoughtful, Penelope deserved attention. I listened more closely.

"Lots of credit to Miss Martinez," Laws said. "Thanks to her background in both music and art, she's helped me with two significant projects. First, she's trained two fine young men who from now on will take turns playing the 'Call-to-the-Colors' every morning—live—on their trumpets. No more recordings. All business will come to a halt while they play and we pay tribute to our nation's flag."

A scattering of applause followed this patriotic news. I wondered if Laws might hire Jeremy Goodman full time if the sub promised to wear his army uniform every day.

"We also have Penelope to thank for a second contribution, a beautiful work of art that I've been dreaming of for many years." Laws motioned for a smiling Mrs. Nichols to bring him the large, white cardboard poster that was lying face down on top of the wooden card catalogue to his left. To maintain secrecy, the obviously rehearsed librarian carried the cardboard before her with its blank side facing out so you couldn't see the front.

"I present to you all," Laws announced as Mrs. Nichols placed the poster in the principal's hands, "the new David Graham Phillips Junior High School coat-of-arms." With those words, he turned the cardboard around and raised it above his head. There for all to see was a line-drawing in black marker of a blue-and-red, medieval-like shield, a simple recreation of old-fashioned heraldry

200

containing what were clearly intended as iconic images.

Breathing heavily, his white-shirted paunch particularly prominent beneath the meager string tie, Laws continued to hold the drawing aloft. "Penelope did the artwork per my instructions," he said between quick breaths. "Eventually, we'll have the design transferred to cloth. Then we'll hang it as a banner in the main stairwell where students and visitors will be able to see it flying proudly."

To ease the strain, Laws lowered the poster and stood it upright on the podium next to him. "Notice the symbolism," he said, waving his free hand at the various components as he described them.

A horizontal stripe split the shield across the middle, separating the top blue section from the bottom portion colored red. A vertical line divided the blue area into two equal parts. The section on the left contained the drawing of an American eagle; the one on the right, a classic scale of justice. An open book filled the lower area, which Laws pointed to in particular. "The book," he said with obvious satisfaction, "represents our namesake—the writer, David Graham Phillips."

He stood for a moment longer to admire Penelope's handiwork and then, holding the poster in both hands, gently laid it (drawing face-up this time) on top of a small bookshelf behind him. "How proud our students will be," he said upon returning to the podium, "when they see our coat-of-arms hanging above them in the stairwell. Years from now they'll remember it. We're starting a tradition today—think of those old British schools like Harrow and Eton."

"The only 'eatin'' he knows about," muttered Frick from somewhere behind me, "is done with a knife and fork."

"Shhhhhhhhhhhhhhhhhhh!" hissed Tiffany Schwartz. Suddenly, she realized she had just addressed the woodshop teacher the way she would one of her students, and her face turned crimson. She fluffed her black hair self-consciously and giggled softly. She may simply have been embarrassed; then again, she might actually have appreciated Frick's humor.

Next up was Mrs. Steele and her predictable instructions for ordering textbooks. Only this time around, her speech felt even more mindless than usual. She must have known how badly Laws had treated Mandy, and yet the woman could just push on, parroting procedures that most in her audience could recite from memory while one of her teachers was getting her career derailed. How could Mrs. Steel tolerate working for the man? How could any of Laws's inner circle support him?

From left to right, I examined the four administrators seated up front—Steele, Swett, Norovsky. And Vivian Laws himself. At some point in their careers, each of them had to make the decision to leave the classroom and walk away from teaching. I could only assume that the more distance

202

they put between themselves and actual teaching, the more guiltless—and happier—they felt.

The meeting droned on for close to two hours as each administrator addressed the faculty. But just as Abe Norovsky, the final speaker, was returning to his seat, one of the double doors in the back of the library opened, and I was shocked to see Mandy walk in. I couldn't imagine what had brought her back from the Fort, let alone how she had returned so quickly. Her expressionless features offered no hint of what she was doing at Phillips or how she felt about being there.

With no empty chairs nearby, Mandy had to stand just inside the library doors and wait until the meeting ended. To hurry the proceedings along, I cut short my comments concerning union membership. Yet even after Laws dismissed us, I didn't get an immediate explanation from Mandy.

I met her at the doorway, but it was obvious that she needed to talk to the principal. Heading towards the podium, she shook her head when I tried to say something. I pointed in the direction of my classroom to indicate where I'd be waiting. As I left the library, I had just enough time to watch Mandy approach Laws's scowling face.

Preparing my room for the new year was the last thing on my mind. For some ten minutes I sat staring at the countless staple holes in the bare bulletin boards waiting for Mandy to come in and announce her fate.

When she arrived, she said, "They told me downtown that Phillips is where I'm assigned and that Phillips is where I'm supposed to stay."

"But Laws—"

"I know, Art." There was an edge to her voice. "That's what I just reported to him, and he wasn't too happy about it. He said it was all a mistake and that I'm still going to get moved."

"Oh, yeah?" I said, sounding like a kid squaring off for a fight in the schoolyard. "Listen. I'm your union rep; it's time for me to get into the act and protect your job." Shoving back my chair, I got to my feet and pushed open the door.

"Wait," Mandy called. "Maybe you're acting just the way Mr. Laws wants. Maybe he's trying to get you to do something foolish."

I turned to face her. "This isn't about me, Mandy; it's about what he's doing to you." Then I rushed off.

As I was marching down the hall, I barely heard her say, "Think about it, Art. Maybe it really *is* about you."

I had no patience to consider her words. My pulse was racing, and I was too busy mapping strategy on the fly. I already knew that Mandy had seniority on her side—that Harry Barnes, who'd arrived the previous semester, had been hired well after she had. I also knew that in light of the strength the teachers had shown during the strike, the Board

204

of Education was taking union complaints more seriously.

The door to Laws's office was open, but he was preoccupied with paperwork and didn't bother to look up. I knocked loudly on the door frame and waited for him to notice me. When he failed to do so, I walked right in. Though his black suit rendered him appropriately grim, his tone was upbeat. "What do you think of it?" he asked, pointing proudly to the school's new coat-of-arms now propped up on the bookshelf behind him.

To be honest, I hadn't noticed the thing. Why should I? I nodded to be polite, then cut to the heart of the matter. "Mr. Laws, I'm here in my capacity as union rep. There's a personnel issue that I need to speak to you about. It concerns Amanda Sayer." My pulse raced all the more as I said her name.

"Oh, yes?" A smirk flickered across the principal's face. "Actually," he said, twisting one end of his string tie with the hand that was missing the finger, "I was expecting you. I believe I also detected your influence last year in Miss Sayer's response to her final evaluation."

"No, sir," I said, trying hard not to let my feelings show, "that was all her own work. But now it's old news."

Laws merely shrugged.

"What is the point," I said, plowing forward, "is that she's been re-assigned here. She has a contract to work at Phillips. That makes you duty-bound not to release her until you've let go any other teachers in her field who have less seniority than she does."

I felt bad bringing up the seniority issue. It put Harry Barnes in the crosshairs, and he was an innocent in all this. I may have been just a kid during the McCarthy era, but I'd learned enough to know that I wasn't going to be the one who'd name names.

"Art," Laws said, letting go of the tie and thrusting both hands outward, palms up, as if in appeal, "this whole thing has been a mix-up from the get-go. As I'm sure you're already aware, Miss Sayer wasn't supposed to have been re-assigned here in the first place. It was the board's error; I have nothing against her personally."

"But she is here," I reminded him with more authority than I was used to employing in the principal's office. This wasn't Janice Storm I was disagreeing with. This was my boss—my vindictive boss. "Don't you forget," I blurted out angrily, "that she has more seniority than Harry Barnes."

Just what I wasn't going to say.

Laws grinned. At some level he must have recognized that by giving up Barnes, I'd gone way farther than I'd intended.

Still, I refused to be put off. "If Miss Sayer were unassigned to a school," I said, "it would be different. But she has a contract, and she's been officially re-assigned to Phillips, and the union will watch closely that you keep her here."

"Thanks for advising me, Mr. Malamud," Vivian Laws said. I couldn't tell if he was being sarcastic. I did get the message, however, when he stood up and showed me the door.

Chapter Fifteen

Adrift

*I*t seemed senseless to me. Credentialed in social studies, Mandy was assigned to teach only English classes. Even if you assumed that Laws was planning to let her go, having Mandy teach outside her field wasn't fair to the students—let alone to Mandy herself.

Then again, it hadn't been fair for Laws to close down the music department a few years earlier to eliminate that teacher he didn't like. Or to have transferred the experienced Mike Falstaff over a dispute about grades. What Jack had said about Falstaff seemed sadly relevant to Mandy: "If they can't fire you fair and square, they try to make you quit on your own."

But Vivian Laws was greatly mistaken if he thought that giving Mandy unfamiliar courses to teach could wear her down.

"Actually," she said after a few days of teaching ninth-grade English, "it's kind of fun doing short stories. The kids get into them. Shirley Jackson and Poe are crowd-pleasers. And it's not so different from what I usually do anyway—teaching history is telling stories too."

I was happy to hear her adjusting so well during those first few days, and I offered to answer any questions she had about teaching grammar or grading essays. When she got around to the distinctions between *lie* and *lay* and *who* and *whom*, we found ourselves doing more talking at home about English than about ourselves.

"The both of you," Jack said to us a couple of days later in the parking lot, "leave your work at school. There's way too much of the year left to be exhausted this early."

His advice was well-intended, but I knew that it wasn't the job that was wearing us down. No matter how good Mandy was at teaching English, she wasn't contracted in the subject, and her position remained precarious. Both of us understood that sooner or later the axe was going to fall. It was simply a question of timing: when was she going to be removed from Phillips and where would she be sent to next?

By the time we arrived home on the second Wednesday of the new semester, the afternoon sunlight had just reached the narrow walkway between our apartment and Mrs. Gross's building in the front. As a result, the shadow of the crabapple tree seemed to be pointing ominously at the black, metal mailbox by the stairs leading up to our place.

In the sunlight you didn't have to open the box to see if any mail had been left inside; the top of its flip-down lid had somehow been bent upward before I'd ever moved in; and if the light was right, you could simply peer down into it and see what was there.

When I first glanced into the box, I thought it was empty. Upon closer examination, however, Mandy spied another one of those small pink notices from the school board stuck at the bottom. She fished the thing out and discovered that, like its predecessor, this one too announced a registered letter being held for her at the post office. Only on this occasion, we had little doubt about its contents.

Once again, we drove to the post office. With her teeth clenched and her gaze straight ahead, Mandy uttered not a word during the short ride. I double-parked next to the flag pole at the center of the parking lot, and Mandy ran inside.

She was already reading the letter when she came out minutes later. By the time she reached the car, her lower lip was trembling.

"I don't believe this," she murmured. Then she said it louder: "Oh, I don't believe this."

I stared at her as she climbed in. "Where are they sending you?"

"They're not sending me anywhere." Her voice was almost a whisper. "They've rescinded my contract."

The enormity of the move caught me by surprise. "Wait," I exclaimed after taking a moment to collect my thoughts, "They can't do that. A contract's a binding agreement. You signed the thing. They can't just rescind it."

She read the page again as if she might have been mistaken, then swallowed hard. "The letter says, 'The board was in error to have originally granted you a second-year contract.' So now they're taking it back."

The blast of a car horn from behind made us jump. We were sitting in the middle of the parking lot, and I had to move. I hit the gas too hard, and the tires of the Dart screeched like yelping dogs.

"Listen to this," Mandy said. As I drove, she read from the letter: "'Implementation of a second-year probationary contract requires the approval of the school supervisor. Your principal has submitted a re-evaluation of your work for last year and has recommended against your advancement.'"

"What re-evaluation?" I asked. "I never heard of any such thing. Did you?"

"No," she said, looking up. "Laws hasn't come into my classroom once this semester. None of the administrators have." Mandy continued to skim the page. "It goes on," she said. "'I am therefore rescinding the probationary contract which generally follows a successful first year of teaching.' The letter's signed by Dr. Homer Thompson."

"Bastards," I muttered, "all of them."

"And get this, Art. It says, 'You may continue employment in the district as a substitute teacher until you are eligible for a new probationary contract in—'" here she faltered "'—in two years.' Two years. It's not fair."

A traffic light turned red, and I slowed to a stop. It gave me a chance to remember. I'd told Laws that he couldn't get rid of Mandy as long as she had a contract. Clearly, the technicality of a legal document wasn't about to stop the man. Vivian Laws had manipulated the board into pulling Mandy's contract.

"We'll talk to the union," I said. Angry as I was, it was the only practical advice I could think of.

Janice Storm had told us to try her at home if anything serious developed. As soon as we got back to the apartment, Mandy sat at the desk and dialed her number. I could only pace back and forth.

The phone conversation started civilly enough, but almost immediately Mandy's tone changed. "No, I really do not think this can wait till tomorrow. I'm losing my contract now. You know— my job?"

Through cupped hands, I shouted, "The contract *Janice* assured us you'd get." I hoped I was loud enough for Janice to hear. I wanted her to know that I regarded the union's incompetence as responsible for the fix Mandy was in.

Mandy shook her fist to shut me up. Okay, maybe I'd gone too far. This was Mandy's fight, and as much as I wanted to yell at somebody, I needed to back off.

Mandy told Janice about the letter from the board. As she listened to Janice's response, she nodded a few times and ran a hand through her long, red hair. Then she listened some more, mumbled thanks, and hung up.

"Let me guess," I said. "She repeated what the union always says: 'Do what they tell you so you won't get dinged for defiance.'"

Mandy nodded. "She also said I should return to Phillips tomorrow. Mr. Laws will probably know the district's intentions by then, and I should go wherever they send me."

"Great union," I said sarcastically, feeling guilty all the while that I was one of its school-site representatives.

"Here's another thing that'll bug you. Janice admitted that Mr. Laws must have been correct last year—you know, when he warned me that his evaluation really could hurt my chances of getting a contract. 'I guess your principal made the right call,' was the way she put it."

"Just great. And the union's behind you a hundred percent, right?"

"Yes," Mandy sighed, folding her hands on the desk, "she said that too. She said to have faith— she said the board can't just take away a contract somebody's accepted in good faith. She said the whole situation's ridiculous."

"Amateurs," I exclaimed. "Remember her plan to go after Laws for not saying anything nice about teachers? I'm sure she didn't follow through on that either. And now this."

🎓

Vivian Laws flashed his teeth in the sliver of a grin that began and ended at his lips. "Did you receive the letter from the board?" he asked Mandy when we entered the main office the next morning.

"Yes," she said, "I got the letter."

"Good. Then we can talk." He looked at me and added, "All three of us can talk."

No sooner were we seated in his office than Laws got directly to the point. "I'm afraid, Miss Sayer, that you'll have to be leaving us. There's really nothing I can do. Downtown has its rules." He was directing his words at Mandy, but at the same time he was sneaking glances at me. "As far as I'm concerned, Miss Sayer, the board's ruling is final. Quite frankly, I'm afraid there isn't any place for you here at Phillips. I assume that the makeshift assignment of English classes we were forced to create for you illustrated our predicament."

"What about the re-evaluation mentioned in the letter?" I asked. "When did that take place?" I was demanding more than asking, but Laws must have felt so triumphant that he didn't mind my tone.

In fact, the principal seemed to be enjoying the one-sided combat.

"That re-evaluation," he said, his voice full of confidence, "is actually protection for the employee, for Miss Sayer here. The board double-checks to be sure the teacher in question isn't being harassed."

The thing was, Mandy and I both knew that there had been no re-evaluation because there had been no additional visits to her classroom by Laws or by any of his underlings. Nor had she received any new evaluation forms or official suggestions related to improving her work. Somehow the man had played the system.

My suspicion must have been evident because Laws said, "Oh, it's very informal. Nothing in writing, you understand. All taken care of on the phone. Downtown only called to verify that the rating she got from me last year was accurate. You know, Art," he said, fixing me with his dark eyes, "I did try to warn your union lady, that Mrs. Storm."

"Where am I to go?" Mandy asked. She spoke with little expression.

Laws cleared his throat. "You've been assigned to the substitute division. You'll be getting calls each day to report to various schools in the district. You might also be interested to know that I took the liberty to speak with the principal at Carnegie. I recommended you as a promising young teacher."

Carnegie—the same junior high Mike Falstaff was exiled to, the same junior high reputed to be the district's dumping ground.

"Don't thank me just yet, however," Laws said. "There'd have to be an opening for you to get placed there." Laws concluded by reminding Mandy that today, Thursday, would be her last at Phillips. Then he stood up and dismissed us.

Mandy and I put off speaking to each other until we were well away from the office. Out in the hallway just inside the school's entrance seemed safe enough.

"If he doesn't think I'm a good enough teacher to stay here," she asked, "why would he recommend me to another school—even one as bad as Carnegie?"

My answer was less than encouraging. "Remember what Jack said? Laws probably hopes that working at a place like that will get you to quit on your own."

"You know what?" Mandy said, "Who even cares?" Suddenly, her voice dropped. "All I know is that right now I have to go to class and teach a bunch of kids I'm never going to see again. Do you really—"

A piercing blast interrupted her, and we both jumped. Not four feet away, just on the other side of the red front doors, stood a boy in a khaki uniform decked out in a blue beret and red sash. We could see him through the windows in the door. At his lips was a shiny trumpet, its bell-shaped horn reflecting an explosion of sunlight. It was Day One of Vivian Laws's "live" "Call to the colors."

⬛

After school, I helped Mandy carry her stuff out to the Dart. Cardboard boxes filled with old books, black and red pens, tests and assignments printed in purple ink—the detritus of a displaced teacher—consequential one day, meaningless the next. Her rolled-up ink drawings and tiny electric trains were last to go into the trunk.

Some kid, one of Mandy's students it so happened, approached us just as I slammed the trunk shut. He was wearing jeans and a light-blue tee shirt with "Power to the People" splayed in red across the front.

"I heard you were leaving, Miss Sayer," he said. "That true?"

"I have to go to another school," she answered diplomatically. "Remember when we studied bureaucracies? You understand all that."

"Yeah," he nodded. "Even so, it stinks. You made me like history."

"Thanks," she said. Mandy savored the compliment all the way back to our apartment. The glow seemed to wane, however, once we started carrying her boxes up the metal staircase and into the living room.

Chapter Sixteen

Purgatory I

I know there are people who like to sub. Jeremy Goodman was forever praising substitute-teaching for its lack of specific responsibilities. "You don't have to take papers home," he'd say. "You don't have to fake interest in students or colleagues. You get the fun of working in a different school each day, and you get paid for vacations if you work often enough. What's not to like?"

Although it's a job I never wanted any part of, traditional classroom teachers are occasionally called upon to cover for absent colleagues, and thus I too had a passing familiarity with the challenges Mandy was going to face. By far, the toughest part of subbing is not knowing the kids. If you can't identify a student by name, you lose a significant tool. There's also that feeling of impotence you get from having to depend on the original teacher's unfamiliar lessons—if any are left for the sub in the first place.

And that's not to mention the disrespect so often shown to subs by students. Woe to the sub who doesn't adhere to the opinion of at least one of my students: "A good sub lets kids do whatever they want." Jeremy himself told of subbing in a class when kids hurled paper wads at him as they left the room. "Could have been worse, man," he said. "Could have been rocks. Or bullets."

Not in my wildest imaginings, however, did I ever stop to consider what full-time subs confront beyond the classroom. While I'd seen them treated as outsiders by the Phillips faculty—ignored at meetings or in hallways or in the cafeteria—I confess to never having thought about the endless wait for those early-morning phone calls that determine what life is going to be like on any given day.

I never thought about it, that is, until I witnessed those mornings following Mandy's dismissal from Phillips when she waited so anxiously for the call from the sub desk that was supposed to tell her where she'd be going to work that day. My own stomach grew tight as I found myself anticipating the ring of the phone.

It was during those early-morning hours— while she lay on her back with her eyes wide open, her body rigid, and her fingers fussing with the top sheet—that I learned the only sound worse than the clamor of an early-morning alarm clock was the uncanny stillness of a stagnating silence: no call, no work, no salary. No interest.

Nor did it ever cross my mind that anyone might purposely attempt to block a sub from working the number of days needed to qualify for vacation pay. Yet that is exactly what the result would be if some mean-spirited administrator simply neglected to submit the sub's name to the assignment desk in the first place. Without resorting to any kind of Byzantine trickery, if enough people in high positions didn't want you to acquire the requisite number of days, then your phone wouldn't ring, and you'd be out the extra money.

The fact that Mandy didn't want to sub in the first place made matters that much worse. As she waited for the phone to ring during that third week of the semester, she had plenty of time to think about the days she wasn't getting credit for. Actually, it took most all of a week's staying in bed and watching TV to demoralize her. By the time I'd get home, she seldom wanted to talk. We were used to having a glass of wine together before making dinner, but during that week she wanted little to do with socializing.

By Friday, however, she couldn't stand it any longer. I'd just finished breakfast; and when I returned to the bedroom, I discovered her sitting upright in bed, her red hair draped over the shoulders of the long, powder-blue tee shirt she slept in.

"Enough," she announced. "This is ridiculous. I'm calling the sub desk to find out why I haven't gotten any assignments."

"Good," I said on my way to the shower. Finally, she was taking matters into her own hands.

By the time I came back, she'd already laid out her teaching clothes on the bed—a white blouse, a blue-denim skirt, and green sweater.

"What gives?"

"Remember when Laws said he was going to put me on the sub list?"

"Yeah," I said, pulling on my jeans.

"Well, he didn't. The sub desk said they've never heard of me."

I looked at her in shock.

"But I insisted they check, and they finally found my name somewhere. And guess what," she announced, green eyes gleaming, "I've got a job today." Suddenly, her entire being was filled with animation. "They're sending me to Paine." She actually clapped her hands together in excitement. "Do you remember? I interviewed there before I came to Phillips."

By the end of the fourth week, Mandy was subbing every day.

"It's not so bad," she said. "I come on strong at the beginning, hand out work-sheets, and the kids fall in line."

Work-sheets—a far cry from the colorful maps and electric trains of the year before. Still, I marveled at her adaptability.

"But don't think that just because things are going well for me now, I'm giving up my battle for what's right."

"We miss you at Phillips," I told her. "Jack and Betty are always asking how you're doing."

"I miss them too. But that doesn't mean I want to go back there. I refuse to work for Vivian Laws. He cost me a lot more than just a school. I want my contract reinstated—along with the second-year salary and security that go with it."

So strongly did Mandy insist on recovering what the district had stolen from her that whenever I discovered she wasn't at the apartment at the end of a school day, I assumed she was out somewhere dealing with her teaching status.

On Thursday of the following week, I was preparing a salad when she got home.

"I went to see Sam Woods at the union this afternoon," she said. "Janice Storm set it up for me."

Sam Woods was the union's director of legal affairs whom I'd pointed out to Mandy at the Olympic during the strike. Like many an astute lawyer, the prickly octogenarian had the reputation for taking on only those cases he felt he had a good chance of winning; the others he tended to ignore— great for the union, not so much for the individual teachers involved or for the ideals they might have been trying to uphold.

"How'd it go?" I asked as I tossed a bunch of lettuce into a large wooden bowl.

"It was my first trip to union headquarters. To tell you the truth, the whole place is underwhelming."

I nodded as I got out the cutting board. I knew what she meant. I'd been to union headquarters a few times to pick up flyers, and in general the scene was pretty drab.

It's located in a gray, three-story office building on Wilshire about halfway between Phillips and downtown. In its former life, the building had belonged to an insurance company.

"You know," she said, "if it weren't for the small, gold lettering on the glass doors that say *Federation of Public-School Teachers*, I couldn't tell that the people inside have the responsibility to defend us."

"Yeah," I nodded. "I remember a small eucalyptus tree standing all by itself near the entrance; it's always reminded me of some poor teacher demanding justice."

"Speaking of which," Mandy said, "a woman at the front desk directed me down a dark hallway to Woods's office. The door was open a crack, so I walked in. Get this. He's at his desk wearing jeans and a red-plaid Pendleton, and he's leaning back in a brown-leather recliner."

"Just like us at school," I joked.

"Yeah, right," Mandy said, "but I'm not done yet. His hands were locked behind his long white hair, and his feet—in golden-brown work boots, no less—were propped up on the desk. If his eyes hadn't been open, I would have sworn he was asleep."

"I'm sure he wasn't," I said, beginning to slice a few mushrooms.

"No. But there wasn't any hello or welcome. He just pointed with his elbow where he wanted me to sit. 'Inform me of your situation, Miss Sayer,' he said."

"At least he knew your name. That's something."

"Yes, I'm sure Janice filled him in on some of the stuff, but even so I told him all about my evaluations. He never moved, not until I got to the part about losing my contract—well, you should have seen him then." Here Mandy waved her arms in imitation of the action she was describing. "He whipped his hands down from behind his head, jerked his feet off the desk, lurched forward in the chair, and wound up with his fingers clasped and his eyes aimed directly at me."

I laughed. "Probably, a move he practices. So what did he have to say? Anything helpful?"

"Long story short, he wanted to file a grievance."

"Really." I stopped slicing. "Just like that?"

"He even raised his fist," Mandy mimicked Woods again, "and said, 'We're going to get that s.o.b.'"

"Wait a minute. You said, 'He *wanted* to file a grievance.' Past tense—that doesn't sound so good."

Mandy pointed her finger at me like a gun. "Right you are. In fact, he actually took a second or two to reconsider my situation. I mean, only minutes before, he'd been talking about filing a grievance."

"So, what happened?"

She shook her head. "He started coming up with reasons for not going ahead with it. First, he warned me how dangerous filing a grievance is. He said that if you lose, the board will always be on your case."

"Ridiculous," I said, dicing some red onion.

"Then, he said, even if you win, you can forget about good schools, good classes, or deserved promotions. You'll be labeled a trouble-maker forever after."

I stopped dicing. "That's B.S. There are plenty of teachers who've filed grievances and won—and gone happily about their business afterwards."

"I'm sure there are," Mandy said. "So there must be some other reason. Maybe I'm thinking too much like you, Art, but the man's negative attitude seemed so, so inevitable—comical, almost."

"I think he faces a problem," I said, pointing the knife in her direction. "If he fights to get your contract back, he'll be opposing the legal language that the union agreed to after the strike—including that bit about how you can't get a contract with a less-than-satisfactory rating."

"But I'm not fighting their legal language. I'm fighting because I lost a contract that I'd accepted in good faith. It's different."

"Agreed. But I'm telling you that as long as Woods thinks that what you want undermines the contract he helped create he's not particularly interested in taking up the fight."

Mandy sighed. "I get what you're saying. It's not a battle the union's going to help me win."

"Right. So did he come up with any other ideas?"

"I was getting to that. He suggested that I go to the Fort and meet with Dr. Thompson. You know, the guy who sent me the letter rescinding my contract."

"Just great," I said. "They want you to go see the guy that caused the trouble in the first place. I'm surprised Woods didn't tell you to go back to Laws on your knees and beg for mercy. What a bunch of amateurs."

"Give it a rest, Art. I'm the one getting shafted, not you."

Mandy was right. It was she who faced the problem, not me. "Sorry," I said, putting down the knife.

Mandy pushed the wooden bowl in my direction, and I slid the chopped veggies into it. I added some leftover chicken and sprinkled a few drops of vinaigrette on top.

"Let's eat," I said and carried the salad to the table.

Mandy set up an appointment with Dr. Thompson for after school the following week.

Although she knew that I still considered appealing to a district administrator counter-productive, she asked me to come along anyway. After all, I was the original union rep in the case.

To get a reading of the situation, I called Janice Storm. Fully expecting her to deliver the company line, I nonetheless thought that hearing her opinion might be worth a shot as she remained my only contact at the union.

"If Sam told Amanda to go see Thompson," Janice said, "then Amanda should go and see the man. I can assure you that if Sam says there's no point in filing a grievance, then—"

"I know—then there's no point in filing a grievance. I get it." I figured Janice realized how pissed off I was; otherwise, she wouldn't have followed up with a near confession concerning her own mishandling of Mandy's case.

"From now on, Art," she said, "I'm going to be sure I read the contract more carefully. I'm not going to let what happened to Amanda happen to any other new teacher."

I suppose that adding her personal mea culpa to the mix was intended to make Mandy's dilemma more palatable. I didn't think that it did.

Chapter Seventeen

Downtown

Mandy met up with me at the front entrance of school-district headquarters, the relatively new, five-story building surrounded by a square of massive gray-brick some eight feet high. "I know they called the old district office 'the Fort,'" she said, clutching papers in one hand and pointing at the enclosing walls with the other. "But one look at this place and you can see why the name has stuck around. It's built like a fortress."

She was right about that. Maybe it was the Vietnam War that seemed to color everything, but the military feel of the new building was difficult to ignore. Whether the architects who designed the place planned it that way or not, they wound up creating what most people would consider an impregnable-looking complex. That is, if those people could ignore the waffle-like array of air conditioners that decorate the outside of the building from the ground floor to the roof—highly coveted appliances, I should add, not then available to most schools in the district.

In the end, however, you have to wonder whether those same architects might have come to regret the martial aspect of the place. In the center of the square, they reversed direction and provided a courtyard of soft grass and leafy ficus trees, complete with rustic wooden benches and tables. It was through the shade of that center quad, in fact, that Mandy and I hustled to make her 4:15 appointment. Together we cut across the lawn to the farthest corner of the complex.

A secretary ushered us into Dr. Thompson's office. The superintendent of teacher placement was a tall, wiry Black man in a dark silk suit. He had short, graying hair and a thick moustache. Half-lens reading glasses gave him a scholarly look, but did little to mask the sadness in his eyes.

Earlier in the day, Jack had furnished me with background on Homer Thompson. "He's got the reputation for being fair," Jack had said. "He suffered a heart attack a couple of years ago when he was only forty-nine—the curse of being a sensitive administrator."

"Stress, no doubt," I said.

Jack agreed. "Word is, he had hopes of becoming superintendent of the entire district, but his heart condition forced him to drop the idea. Other people think he just got fed up."

Whatever the cause of Thompson's woes, Jack's description seemed apt enough. The man rose when we entered, but he looked weary. The furrows that lined his features suggested not only someone who'd heard every sob story related to institutional stupidity that a teacher had to tell, but also someone unable to understand why such senselessness couldn't be rooted out before it ever took hold.

We introduced ourselves—Mandy as the aggrieved party, I as the Phillips union rep—and Thompson indicated that we sit in the leather chairs facing his desk.

"What seems to be the problem, Miss Sayer?" he asked in a high-pitched voice.

Mandy repeated her unhappy history with Vivian Laws; and Thompson, peering at her over the straight edges of his half-glasses, listened patiently. When she finished, she presented Thompson with the papers she'd brought to back up her account: Laws's first evaluation (the relatively acceptable one), Laws's second evaluation (the intolerable one), her own rebuttal, the lesson plans with Sam Turner's compliments written in red marker across the top, and the now-voided probationary contract offering her employment. She concluded dramatically enough by displaying the letter from the board that had rescinded her contract, the letter signed by the very man facing us across his highly polished desktop.

Thompson proceeded to riffle through the material, paying particular attention to Laws's two contradictory reviews. When the superintendent was done, he gathered all the pages together and squared them up on the shiny desktop. He peered at Mandy once more and said, "You make a very strong case for yourself, Miss Sayer."

"Thank you, sir," she smiled appreciatively.

"And yet your evidence is incomplete."

Mandy and I exchanged questioning looks.

Thompson opened a desk drawer and pulled out a printed form, which displayed the circular district-logo at the top. He slid the page across the polished desktop towards Mandy.

I got up to read over her shoulder, and I immediately saw Laws's signature at the bottom of the printed form. With the same summary box checked, it looked identical to the last evaluation he'd given Mandy.

"That," Thompson said, "is the re-evaluation form which your principal was required to complete. You'll note that once again he's checked 'below standard performance.' Otherwise, we would never have considered so drastic a measure as revoking your contract."

I sat down slowly as Thompson held up the last page Mandy had given him.

"In truth," he said, fluttering the paper, "this letter you received from me made reference to that very re-evaluation. That's why I'm surprised you don't have a copy."

"We've never seen it," I told Thompson. "Laws said that the re-evaluation was informal. He said all he did was talk to someone on the phone."

"I believe," Mandy added, "his exact words were, 'Nothing in writing.'"

"That's right," I said. "According to Laws, all he was doing was agreeing with last year's evaluation."

Thompson cocked an eyebrow as he took back the form.

"That new review is bogus," I said, my voice rising in irritation. "The man hasn't been back to Mandy's—Miss Sayer's—classroom since he gave her his first review. He has absolutely no way of knowing if she's 'corrected'"—I made air-quotes to demonstrate my disdain—"any of his so-called complaints."

Thompson let out his breath. "What can I say?" he asked, looking at Mandy. "We here at the board, Miss Sayer, would have been quite content to let you keep your contract. Consider the additional paperwork, if nothing else. Not to mention the displeasure of the teacher—you, in this case."

Mandy smiled at the concession.

"We sent your principal the re-evaluation form," Thompson continued, "with the hope he'd say, 'Forget the whole thing.' I certainly wish he had. But, you see, ultimately, the final decision was up to him."

"If that's really true,'" I said, "then why did you have to send him a re-evaluation form in the first place? Why couldn't he just have kicked Miss Sayer out on his own? With due respect, sir, if the decision really was his to make, why did he need your permission at all?"

Thompson shook his head. "You seem to misunderstand the situation, Mr. Malamud. Believe me, we were not the party that initiated the action. Mr. Laws was the one who notified us of Miss Sayer's return to Phillips. It was he who prodded us to begin the proceedings, not the other way around."

"Do you mean to tell me," Mandy said, her brow furrowed, "that if I'd been assigned to some other school and not had to see Mr. Laws this September, I wouldn't have lost my contract?"

"Precisely," Thompson nodded as he squared up Mandy's papers again. "If you hadn't turned up at Phillips, Mr. Laws would have had no reason to contact us. I'm sure both of you can appreciate that in an organization as large as this, many things go unnoticed."

Quite the understatement, I thought.

But Thompson wasn't finished. "I should add," he said, holding up Mandy's papers, "that—off the record, of course—from what I've seen here, had your principal's criticism of Miss Sayer gone undetected, it would no doubt have been for the best. In short, Miss Sayer, I think you got a raw deal."

Mandy looked at the superintendent with obvious respect. "If you really do believe that, sir," she said, "what can be done to rectify the situation?"

"First," Thompson said, "I'll have to talk with Mr. Woods at the union." Turning to me, he said, "As you union reps are aware, ever since the strike settlement, the district and the union have to agree on just about everything."

233

Pleased to learn the strike had some positive effect, I leaned back and flashed a smile.

Thompson remained silent for a moment, knitting his brows as if in deliberation with himself. Then he addressed Mandy. "As I'm sure you recall from my letter, Miss Sayer, ordinarily, a probationary teacher has to wait two years following a negative evaluation before qualifying for a new contract."

The superintendent paused to scan Mandy's papers once more. When he looked up, he said, "But I see no reason that we cannot safely cut that to one. And I think we can also find you a quality school where you'll be able to teach the required two semesters more happily than you might as a substitute in a different location every day."

I didn't really expect Thompson to reverse the evaluation submitted by Vivian Laws—a fellow administrator, after all—and Mandy had already given up the idea of teaching at Phillips. As much as I missed her presence, I couldn't blame her for not wanting to face Laws's wrath every day. There was also the major appeal of teaching at a single good school instead of subbing in lots of strange places all over the city—especially when after one year instead of two she could regain the same contract she had signed just a few months earlier.

Putting aside my own selfish desires to keep Mandy near me, I had to admit that Thompson's proposal sounded pretty good. For a moment I considered objecting to that last bit about her being forced to leave Phillips, but when I felt her fingers digging into my arm, I kept quiet.

"Agreed," Mandy said and offered her hand to Thompson in the time-honored tradition of solidifying a deal. He took it and smiled.

🎓

"What an asshole," I blurted out as soon as we'd left the building.

Mandy stopped short. "Thompson? All things considered, I thought he was quite helpful."

"No, not Thompson," I said, shaking my head. "Laws. He could have let it all blow over, but instead he had to go and notify the board."

Mandy gazed heavenward in exasperation. "Honestly, Art, for all your talk about crooked politicians and the need for unions, you really don't see what's going on here."

"Of course, I do," I said. "Laws thought you were some sort of rebel when you wrote that rebuttal to his evaluation. He sees you as a threat to his authority."

"How convenient," she smiled. "You seem to have forgotten that those classroom observations came before I ever wrote the rebuttal." She cocked an eyebrow. "And yet you still think I'm the one he sees as a threat."

"Laws wanted to teach you a lesson—a new teacher going out on strike."

"Harry Barnes went out, and he's not in any trouble."

She had a point. "Okay. You're right about Barnes." I decided it was time for a more traditional approach. "So maybe Laws doesn't like women. Maybe it's just as simple as that. Remember how uptight he was around his wife at the Christmas party? Frick said he must have 'Unresolved Sexual Problems.'"

Mandy smiled and slowly shook her head. "So now you're quoting Don Frick?"

Even I thought my explanation sounded weak.

"Come on," she said, taking my arm. "Let's get our cars." Although we'd each driven on our own to the board, we'd both left our cars on the ground level of the parking structure. It was in that direction Mandy now guided me. Over the tall gray wall to the west, you could see the sky blazing orange.

When we reached Mandy's VW, she turned to face me. "Art, remember when I told you that maybe this business is really about Laws and you?"

"Me?" I said. "Me? That's ridiculous. I'm not the victim here; you are. This whole enterprise is about your evaluation. I don't see him going after you to get to me. He can call me into his office whenever he wants."

She shook her head. "We were dating when all this started, you know. Now we're living together. You don't have to be too smart to figure out that hurting me will also hurt you."

236

She was right about that too; I guess how involved we were with each other was pretty obvious. But we'd just had a meeting with a superintendent about Mandy's job, not mine. "We can talk more about it at home," I said and kissed her good-bye.

"Yeah, sure," she said and, sounding disappointed, got into her car.

Walking the few rows over to the Dart gave me time to consider Mandy's logic. Her theory still seemed farfetched. Laws never hesitated to criticize me when the opportunity presented itself; he couldn't be so twisted that he'd try to get to me through Mandy. "No way," I muttered and unlocked my car.

I turned on the radio as soon as I started the engine. With the Monkees singing about love and fairy tales, I joined one of the two rows of cars leaving the lot.

Mandy, who'd pulled out before me, had already entered the other line.

As I sat behind the wheel tapping my fingers to the beat of Micky Dolenz's drums, I surprised myself by considering Mandy's explanation some more. Maybe she really was on to something. Maybe Laws really was after me. Maybe he really was that twisted.

I have to confess that the more I thought about it, the more convincing her analysis sounded. After all, I was the one who'd led the Phillips teachers out on strike; I was the one who'd helped Jack with the evaluation forms; I was the one who'd raised the issue of Mandy's contract. As reluctant as I was to accept the idea, in the end I found myself wondering why Vivian Laws wouldn't want to cause me heartbreak?

I pulled my car even with Mandy's just as "I'm a Believer" was finishing on the radio. A quick beep of my horn got her attention. Once she looked my way, I signaled to her that I wanted to talk.

With her left hand still on the wheel and her long red hair falling over her extended right arm, she leaned across the passenger seat and rolled down the window. "What?" she wanted to know.

"I think you're right about Laws," I shouted over to her. "I think I've been naïve."

"Finally," she mouthed and signaled me a thumbs-up. There wasn't much else she could do but drive out of the lot. I followed her into the procession of red tail-lights heading west.

Chapter Eighteen

Hope

*D*espite the turmoil in our personal lives, teaching went on. It was then the fourth week of the new semester, and while I had known from day one that I would be teaching Greek and Roman mythology to my seventh-graders, as a substitute, Mandy couldn't predict the grade or subject she might be addressing each day. As a result, she was constantly reviewing various history texts to come up with generic social studies assignments that would fit whatever level of students she might be assigned to teach.

Which is not to say that Mandy had given up on her personal war with the school district. The day after our meeting with Thompson, she told me she'd called the union and learned that, true to his word, Thompson had already informed Sam Woods of the plan to help her. Even better, Woods hadn't complained that reducing Mandy's probationary period would alter the terms of the union's agreement with the district. On the contrary, Woods quickly approved.

"Of course, he likes the deal," I told Mandy at dinner. "It frees the union from responsibility. Not only will he not have to defend you, but he also won't have to argue against the legal language that he himself helped compose."

She nodded and sampled her wine.

I took a drink myself. "You know, if you wanted to sue somebody, rather than cooking up a case against Thompson or even Laws, who were just doing their rotten jobs ..."

"Just following orders," Mandy said.

"Yeah, exactly. If you wanted to sue somebody, I'm thinking a good lawyer could work up a case against the union higher-ups for not defending you better, for not giving you the proper advice on how to keep your position."

"And if I won, do you think I'd get my job back?"

"Not in a million years," I said.

Once he'd received approval from Sam Woods, Superintendent Thompson sent Mandy a list of the few schools that still had openings. Though Thompson had lived up to his promise—the recommended schools seemed to pose few problems—all of them were junior highs. And Mandy, like many a junior high school teacher—myself included, as I had told her—wanted to teach older kids.

"I was hoping for a high school," she said.

"Yeah, so was I. I already told you how that worked out."

In fairness to Mandy, her situation was different from mine. At the start of my career, I had arranged my own interviews. She could only attend those that had been set up for her, and as it turned out—so far, at least—those interviews were only at junior highs. What's more, neither one of us had ever interviewed for a position after a new school year had already started, and thus we could never have predicted the cut-throat competition for teaching jobs that occurs once a semester has begun.

Who knew that an vacant position after September is considered a rare commodity? Principals are constantly on the lookout for teachers to fill last-minute openings. And yet, paradoxically, a teacher who hasn't secured a job by then is viewed with suspicion. "Why aren't you already working?" principals want to know. Even worse, for a young teacher like Mandy, the odds of landing so precious a job favor teacher with experience.

In her sleep, one night after those fruitless interviews had begun, Mandy started grinding her teeth again.

"Wake up, babe," I whispered, gently touching her shoulder.

In the muted moonlight washing through the curtains, I watched her turn in my direction. Without opening her eyes, she instinctively wrapped her arms around me. "Wha—?"

Suddenly, she jerked awake, green eyes wide. "Yesterday, at the interview—the principal—she advised me to wear my hair in a bun. In order to look older. You know—like I do the first day of class. She said it would help my chances of getting hired."

"A junior high school principal," I reminded her, hoping to blunt the criticism.

It was the middle of the night, but Mandy sat up straight. "I just this second realized. It's not 'cause I don't look old enough. That's not the point; it's just the cover story. It's really all that stuff with Laws, which they don't want to admit they know."

"You think?"

"It has to be. It follows me around. Dr. Thompson can say all he wants to about fair play and principals can blather on about looking older, but I think it's just like Laws said—principals talk to each other and know in advance which teachers to avoid hiring."

"Laws told me the same thing in his office," I said. "They talk on the phone. I took it as a warning."

Mandy started folding and unfolding the hem of the sheet. If Thompson hadn't sounded so reassuring when he'd promised he'd get her a job, I do believe she would have given up searching right then.

🎓

In the middle of the fifth week, Mandy had her first interview at a high school—Cooper. Coincidentally, on the same day, my ninth-graders and I finished reading "The Speckled Band," the Sherlock Holmes adventure about a killer-snake. I like teaching the story because the differences between the fictional reptile and real snakes provide me the opportunity to discuss how you shouldn't believe everything you read. Or are told. All the time I was talking to my students about truth, I kept thinking about the promises Superintendent Thompson had made to Mandy.

Once school was over, I hurried back to the apartment eager to find out how Mandy's interview had gone. Yet I slowed my pace as I climbed the metal stairs. Interested as I was, I also feared hearing more bad news.

Wrong again.

"I got it," she screamed, throwing her arms around me as soon as I opened the door. "At Cooper—a high school."

"All right!" I hugged her tightly.

"A history teacher retired at the last minute—that's why there was an opening. And at the end of the interview, Mrs. Sanchez—the principal—she offered me the job. Just like that. She's young, somebody I can relate to. I'm supposed to report on Monday."

"That's great," I exclaimed, "really." I meant it, of course. I too could relate. Burdened with worry over the machinations of Vivian Laws, I welcomed news of a principal who epitomized someone you might be able to count on for help, someone in the school district who represented hope.

All was good; finally, truth had triumphed. The superintendent who'd promised Mandy a decent school had come through. The job at Cooper was supposed to run at least two semesters, the length of time Thompson had said she needed to re-qualify for a contract. The board finally seemed ready to make up for the harassment Mandy had suffered at Phillips.

To celebrate, we went out for dinner. Italian this time.

"And get this," I told Jack and Betty at lunch, "Mandy said that every morning the principal has coffee waiting for the teachers in the main office." I paused a dramatic moment to let them take that in.

Jack nodded, and Betty let out a soft giggle.

"And it gets even better," I said. "She's given Mandy two honors classes and came in to watch her teach during the first week to make sure everything was going all right. Lots of good strokes. Even the kids have been great."

Betty laughed loudly. "I'll bet she's gotten more compliments in one week over there than she got in two semesters here from Laws."

"I know the union rep at Cooper," Jack said. "He used to be a big shot on the union board of directors—until he got interested in teaching again."

"He's her department chair," I said. "Mandy told him her story, and now he's looking out for her."

"Yeah, that sounds right," Jack said. "He's a good guy—lots of years in and out of the classroom."

"Get this," I said. "Mandy asked him about supervision assignments—you know, like the patrolling we do here before and after school. He told her that unless there's some kind of an emergency, they don't do them at all."

"Excellent." Jack smiled broadly.

"Tiffany must be right," Betty said. "We should all be teaching high school."

"Tell me about it," I said.

"I don't agree." Jack rubbed his head. "I like this age. The kids are open, more spontaneous. Wiser people than I have said that a junior high school is where you learn how to teach."

"All I know," Betty said, "is that it's about time Mandy caught a break. Jeremy thinks the same. He said that anybody who's been kicked around the way she has and still wants to teach deserves a medal."

In fact, after a shaky beginning, the semester progressed in a positive direction for all of us. Jack had begun counting the days until his June retirement, and the union had given me little to worry about. Even Vivian Laws seemed to have mellowed. His only reaction to Marc Whisk for leaving a paper-cutter unattended—and thereby allowing a student to sever the tip of his finger—was to call the art teacher "irresponsible." Marc said he was sorry, and we all began to wonder if the "captain" was losing his edge.

Fall became winter, and the holiday traditions kicked in once more. Santa Claus made his annual appearance in our classrooms, and yet again the Norovskys hosted their annual Christmas bash.

Not that we went. No sooner did the invitation arrive than Mandy said, "You can go by yourself if you want, but I won't go anywhere near where Vivian Laws is. I mean it this time."

We skipped the party and, like the year before, enjoyed our winter break hanging out together. Sweetening the holiday was Mandy's paycheck for the vacation. Despite her slow start at subbing, she had taught enough days to qualify for the extra money.

I finished up the fall term for my ninth-graders with *Macbeth*. I read the lead, and for the fight scene at the end I got Betty to come in from next door and play MacDuff. We used yardsticks for swords, and the kids howled.

Mandy ended the semester at Cooper with her history-interview assignment. Mrs. Sanchez observed the class while Mandy was explaining the requirements. "Outstanding work," the principal told her.

Soon thereafter, the fall term concluded, and Mandy and I spent the weekend between semesters in Yosemite.

Chapter Nineteen

Purgatory II

*T*he spring semester began routinely enough, so I had no reason to suspect anything amiss when I saw the folded note inside my mailbox in the main office. It was the middle of the second week, and I figured that some parent had a question about the direction one of my classes was going to take.

In fact, the message came from Mandy, and it read, "Meet me at home." Obviously, she needed to tell me something, which she had no intention of imparting to the student monitor who answered the school phone.

She was sitting at the desk in the apartment when I got there, hands by her side, green eyes staring off at nothing. Her book bag lay on the floor near the couch.

"I got bumped," she said, her tone ice cold. In a word, she'd been replaced by another teacher—presumably, a veteran with the seniority to "bump" a less experienced colleague out the door.

The familiar knot in my stomach—the knot I thought I was rid of once Mandy had gotten the job at Cooper—tightened up just the way it used to.

"Thompson promised you two semesters at the same school," I said, wondering for how long the shadow of Vivian Laws would continue to hang over her. "What's going on?"

She ignored my question. "I like Cooper," she said. "I don't want to leave it. And I certainly don't want to sub again. Ever."

I sat down on the couch. "Tell me what happened."

With little emotion, Mandy reported the details—how Mrs. Sanchez had called her into her office when Mandy arrived at school and told her she had some bad news. The board had sent Mrs. Sanchez a social studies teacher with a contract requiring a position—in short, a teacher for whom the principal was forced to provide a job.

"A 'must-place,' I said. "The needs of the board come first."

Mandy nodded. "Mrs. Sanchez said there was nothing she could do. She said she was really sorry because I'd been doing such a great job."

"Well, at least that's nice to hear."

"I suppose," Mandy said. "Then Mrs. Sanchez asked me to go help the new teacher get started."

I shook my head. "To go help the person who was forcing you out of your job."

The more Mandy related, the sadder she became, especially when she described how the new teacher, who was sitting at Mandy's desk, gave her a dirty look when Mandy came into the classroom.

"What was her problem? You're the one who got bumped. What was bothering her?"

"Can't you guess?" Mandy asked with a wan smile. "It's perfect, really. She didn't want to be there any more than I wanted to leave. Turns out there was a drop in enrollment at her old school in the valley, and they transferred her to this side of the hill. She was pissed because her old school was ten minutes from her house, and now she has to drive across the city."

"So she's getting screwed too. Unbelievable."

"But you'd be proud of me, Art. I asked her when she'd signed her contract. I was thinking that maybe I outranked her seniority-wise."

"Like with Harry Barnes." (As if such an advantage had helped Mandy at Phillips.)

"She told me she'd started teaching this past September—September of this year, Art. I have a full year's seniority on her." Mandy shook her head. "Only I don't—because Laws had the district take back my contract."

"It's so unfair," I said.

"Kids saw me cleaning out my desk, and throughout the day they kept coming up to ask me if it was true that I was leaving, and all I could say was yes." The tone in her voice softened. "I didn't bring anything home. I couldn't get myself to move it all again. I'm too tired to care."

"Don't worry," I told her, hoping I sounded upbeat. "We can pick up your stuff in a couple of days. "What about your union rep? What'd he have to say?"

"I saw him at lunch. He told me to call Sam Woods at the union—the two of them go back a long time."

"Which you intend to do." I meant it as an imperative, but it came out sounding more like a question.

"I guess. But if they want me to sub again . . . ." She put her head down and ran her hands through her red hair. "To be honest—I feel like quitting."

"Don't be silly," I said. "You're too good a teacher to be talking like that."

She looked up. "I don't know, Art. Lately, I've been thinking a lot about it. People keep telling me I'm pretty good at drawing, and you know how I've always wanted to be an architect."

"Yeah, I remember—ever since you drew the picture of the Empire State Building when you were a kid." I looked around at her drawings we'd put up on the walls: The Tower Bridge. The Houses of Parliament. A rendering of the Golden Gate Bridge she'd done after our trip to San Francisco the past summer.

"It's all gotten so complicated," she said. "I just want to be a teacher. Why can't they leave me alone?"

When Mandy woke up the next morning, instead of calling the assignment desk to announce that she was available for subbing again, she said she was going to stay home and work the phone. She'd start with the union. She was ready for a fight.

"I called Sam Woods," she told me when I got back that afternoon. "I told him the rep at Cooper said I should call."

"And?"

She surprised me with a burst of laughter. "Woods got angry when I said I'd been bumped—as if it had happened to him. He shouted into the phone about the commitment Thompson had made to keep me in the same school for a year. Then he asked me if I'd gotten Thompson to put it in writing."

As soon as Mandy spoke the words, I realized that neither one of us had thought of it.

But Mandy wasn't about to accept the blame. "I told him that, no, I didn't get it in writing, and he yelled that I should get everything in writing. 'Aren't you smart enough to know that?' he said. I didn't care for his tone, so I came back at him, 'Aren't you smart enough to have warned me?'"

"Cool," I said, "but we did screw up."

"Maybe so, but you know what?" With a broad grin, she leaned back, raised her arms, and stretched. "It felt good to tell somebody off. Even if it was the person who's supposed to be helping me."

"Some help. Then what happened?"

"He told me to call Thompson. Which I did. I figured I should be telling him I lost my position at Cooper."

"Thompson's been pretty sympathetic. What did he say?"

"Yeah," Mandy smiled, "sympathetic. In the first place, he had only the vaguest recollection of who I even was—let alone recalling our earlier conversation. I had to remind him. I mean, it was a couple of months ago."

"You're too nice."

"He finally did remember, and he said he was sorry—very sorry—to hear I got bumped. After listening to me complain long enough, he repeated that I still needed only one year of successful teaching to earn back my contract. And he agreed that, yes, the new location—wherever that turns out to be—will count as the second of the two semesters."

"Well, that's something,"

"And you know what else?" she smiled. "This time I asked him to put it in writing. You see, I've learned my lesson. I'll be getting a letter in the mail."

"Sam Woods will be pleased," I said. "But what about the future? Did Thompson give you any hints about where they're going to send you?"

"Oh, Thompson's not the person who makes the actual teaching assignments. I learned that as well. Some other guy, another assistant superintendent, somebody named Joe Pontiac, does the assigning. This late into the year, there are no interviews; they just send you wherever there's an opening."

"So, you called the guy?"

"I did. He was polite enough, but he showed little interest in hearing my story. In fact, he cut me off. He told me he didn't make commitments and couldn't even promise I'd end up staying at any one place. All he does is assign. I told him he wasn't very reassuring."

"Everybody passes the buck."

"Well, he asked me if I still wanted him to find me a school; and when I said that I did, he started humming into the phone."

"Like your problem was no big deal?"

"I guess he was looking at some list, but the longer he hummed, the angrier I got. Finally, he said, 'Thomas Paine Junior High.'"

"Paine?" The school where Mandy had subbed the first time and where she'd interviewed before taking the job at Phillips. "At least, you know the place."

"That's true, but you know me—I don't want to go to a junior high. Not after teaching in a high school. I want to go back to Cooper. I feel like I belong there. Besides, I've already spent half my trial year at Cooper; it's not right that I have to give it up."

I couldn't argue with her; she didn't have to sell me on the appeal of teaching at a high school. "So what's your plan?"

"Oh, I'll do what they want me to. I'm supposed to report to Paine tomorrow, and I will. But I'm going to try to get back to Cooper. The only thing is," she said, "the longer I'm at the new place, I just know that the harder it'll be to get out."

All that was left for me to do was nod.

The scene that greeted me when I got home on Mandy's first day at Paine didn't inspire confidence. In jeans and a tee-shirt, her red hair pulled back in a ponytail, she was seated at her easel in a corner of the living room with her hands folded. I hadn't seen the easel for months, not since she'd completed her drawing of the Golden Gate.

Next to the drawing paper on the easel board a color photograph was affixed with a red push pin. It was the picture of Mandy and me that Betty Warden had taken a month earlier in front of Mrs. Gross's apartment building. The two of us were positioned on the sidewalk, and you couldn't see our own apartment from that angle.

As I got closer to the easel, I could see that Mandy had completed the faint outline of the entire composition. The pencil drawing was a realistic recreation of Mrs. Gross's building with its two turrets. Only the people were missing.

I complimented Mandy's artwork, settled into the couch, and waited a minute to work up my nerve. "So, what happened?" I finally asked. "How was it at Paine?"

Mandy picked up her pencil and began to add shadings to her drawing. She worked for a bit, then offered a tired smile. "You know, Art, I hadn't remembered how depressing the place is. It's one of those cold, gray, modern-looking schools. It could be a prison only there aren't any bars, just chain-link fences all around. At least, Phillips has all that red brick to give it some charm."

"The principal's a trip though—Mrs. Flowers." Mandy put down the pencil and turned to face me. "She's a little old Black lady who seems to be famous for wearing pink bedroom slippers—problems with her feet."

"Was she watching everybody come in like Laws does?"

"Not really. She was down the hall when I got there, so I only saw her from a distance. She was talking to the head counselor. He wears a black eye-patch."

"Like a pirate?"

"Or a Cyclops. In any event, I managed to find my department chair, Josephine Purcell. She's the woman who interviewed me last year—"

"Before you came to Phillips."

"Right. I remembered her as nice enough, but back then Phillips felt like a better fit."

Mandy chuckled at that last observation. I couldn't be sure if her laugh was sarcastic.

"Anyway," Mandy said, "she's a serious lady; and she was talking to this enthusiastic, young teacher. Nancy Gold was her name, and for a moment I thought we could be friends. But then Purcell tells her that I'm going to be Nancy's replacement. Nancy Gold was the person I was about to bump."

"And you know how that feels."

"She just stood there with her eyes wide and her mouth open. And then she burst into tears and ran off down the hall."

"Nobody had warned her?"

"In a word, no."

Those are the breaks, I thought. It was too bad, but Mandy, better than most, knew first-hand how the system worked. Especially if you were new. At least, Mandy had a job and the promise of a contract. It made me wonder why she had retreated into drawing.

"So then I go to my new classroom," Mandy said, "and a minute or two later the kids start coming in. They mill around, figuring I'm a sub. The tardy bell hasn't rung yet, and a couple of them keep walking in and out the door. Others are shooting paper wads at the trash. Turns out it's Discussion Day."

"What's that?"

Mandy arched her eyebrows. "Get this. It seems that Miss Gold gives—gave—the kids one period a week to talk about whatever they want. The others, the ones who don't feel like talking—they just hang out with each other or listen to their radios." Mandy folded her arms. "Not my style, I can tell you."

It wasn't mine either.

"But here's the thing, Art. When the bell rang and class actually started, the behavior didn't change. The kids just kept getting up and walking around. Except that they all wanted to know what happened to Miss Gold. Believe me, I laid down the law."

"What'd you do?"

"I told them to sit in their seats and shut up—when you're a sub, you learn a lot about how to handle disruptive classes. I gave them my list of rules and told them there'd be no more Discussion Days. The kids were very unhappy, I can assure you."

Mandy began to draw again as she told the story. Under her quick movements, little round puffs on the paper turned into blooming azalea bushes.

"As you might expect," she said, "they blamed me for getting rid of Miss Gold—for getting rid of their cool teacher."

I shook my head.

"At lunch, I made the mistake of going to the faculty cafeteria, and some of my so-called colleagues actually turned their backs on me. One lady, this big, angry woman, said, 'In case you're interested, Nancy Gold just resigned.'"

Mandy laid down the pencil and this time turned to stare out the window.

The afternoon was growing darker.

I shook my head again. "Do administrators even worry about the effects their chess moves have on teachers—let alone on kids?"

"You're right about that. Still, the news isn't totally depressing. They did give me a couple of honors classes, and that's all to the good."

Mandy got up from her easel and came over and sat next to me. "We haven't had much time together," she whispered. "Maybe when I get back to Cooper, things will change."

Mandy's first weeks at Paine provided numerous horror stories. She would share them with me over afternoon glasses of wine. On one occasion, she sent a kid to the office for hitting a classmate, but only minutes later he reappeared with a message from his counselor—the kid should be taken back into the class because it was Miss Sayer's fault that she couldn't control her students.

The counselor had been wrong on many levels—primarily, for bad-mouthing a teacher to a student, but also for returning a kid to a situation he'd just gotten kicked out of. Yet when Mandy had gone to the head counselor, the one-eyed Warren Greenspan, to question the counseling office's philosophy on sending kids back to class, he brought up an entirely different issue.

He was happy she'd come in, he told her, since he'd been meaning to inform her that it wasn't school policy to give honors classes to new teachers. She should consider herself forewarned that he'd be taking hers away and giving them to the teacher next door—a person who, Mandy learned later, had only begun teaching at the start of the current semester. In terms of seniority, Mandy had been working in the district for well over a year, and she told Greenspan so.

"But in terms of local seniority," the head counselor said, "your neighbor has been at Paine longer than you have."

I didn't know how to react, so I just freshened our drinks.

Two days later, things got worse. When I came home Friday afternoon, I found Mandy sitting at the desk, the telephone receiver at her ear.

"I'm on hold," she said, pointing at the phone. "Superintendent Thompson." Tapping a red pencil on a pad of yellow legal paper, she reported her latest grief to me. "Greenspan came to my classroom during my conference period this morning. He wanted to tell me that as a result of permanent-program day, Paine has to lose two teachers. 'You were the last one in, and you're the first to go,' he said. He told me not to come back on Monday."

I clenched my fists. "But Thompson sent you a letter confirming you'd stay at one school for the rest of the semester. He—"

Mandy held up a finger interrupting my rant. "Yes, I'm still waiting," she said into the telephone and rolled her eyes.

I couldn't believe how calm she was. "How—?"

"I'm better now. At the time, I was speechless. I thought Greenspan was coming in to take away my honors classes, not to break the news that they were letting me go. Then, if you can believe it, he started telling me his own problems—like how much work it was going to be for him to change the students' schedules around because of the loss of teachers."

I shook my head.

"I called downtown as soon as I got back here," Mandy said, still on hold, the phone still at her ear.

"Let me get this straight," I said, my anger continuing to grow, "he—"

Mandy raised her pencil and motioned me to be quiet. "I'm being connected," she whispered. At the same time, she waved me toward the bedroom.

I got the message. She wanted no interference on my part, no yelling at the phone the way I'd done when she'd spoken to Janice Storm about losing the job at Phillips.

I closed the door behind me and began pacing around our bed. I could barely hear Mandy's muffled voice; but while I couldn't make out her words, I could certainly sense the irony. Here she was, trying to save her position at Paine, the very school she'd so recently been fighting to get out of.

I only stopped marching once she came in to announce that the call was over.

"So, what did Thompson say?"

"Get this. He said he was happy to hear from me. He'd just gotten approval from his supervisor that the two semesters at different schools could count as my required year for re-instatement. He said I should be very pleased."

"You're telling me that he didn't know you'd been bumped from Paine?"

"Yep," she smirked.

"So, how'd he handle that news?"

"At first he sounded annoyed, but then—"

I didn't let her finish. "What do you mean, 'annoyed'? At you? You're the innocent the victim in all this."

"At me. At the situation. At having to deal on a Friday afternoon. Who knows?"

I began pacing again.

Mandy sat down on the bed and straightened out the blue afghan next to her so that it formed a smooth seat. "Come over here, Art. You haven't given me a chance to tell you. Thompson did actually fix things."

I settled down next to her and took her hand. "Okay, what?"

"Thompson said he's going to consider me 'off-the-norm' at Paine. I can go back on Monday, and I won't count in the faculty total."

I shook my head once more. "Can he do that?" As soon as the words were out of my mouth, I realized the ridiculousness of my question. "Of course, he can," I answered myself. "He's the board."

"Right," Mandy said. "It's just too bad he didn't think of that when I was forced out of Cooper."

I put my arm around her, and Mandy laid her head on my shoulder. At the very least, she wasn't being chased out of her school. She could stay at Paine. Yet later that night she was grinding her teeth again.

Chapter Twenty

Out of the Ashes

Mandy successfully reclaimed her job at Paine (minus the honors classes). She appreciated all of Superintendent Thompson's efforts, but there was no way she was done fighting for the position at Cooper that she'd been forced out of. Whatever leverage she had, it remained with the union; and at Sam Woods's suggestion, she arranged a meeting with the executive director to see what more could be done.

Mel Avrutin was another one of the big shots we'd seen from a distance during the strike-meeting at the Olympic. He had appeared a mere sidekick of the union president that day, but in reality the executive director possessed more political influence within the union than the president himself. The president had to be elected; Avrutin, a contracted worker, would remain head-of-staff even if the membership voted the president out.

On the night before her meeting with Avrutin, Mandy and I worked together to compile a historical record of her saga. She listed the outrages on a timeline; I converted each event into a short, descriptive paragraph; and Mandy, asserting her editorial rights as needed, employed my Smith Corona electric to type up a final narrative.

"You'll come with me tomorrow afternoon?" she asked. "I mean, you were there at the start of all this. In addition to everything else, I still regard you as my union rep."

"Of course," I said, unable to envision any aid from the union. "Whatever I can do to help."

🎓

Framed in the doorway to his office like a monochromatic photograph, the executive director of the teachers' union stood frozen behind his black-lacquered desk in a gray polyester suit, white shirt, gray tie, and white belt. His thinning gray comb-over didn't muss, and his polyesters didn't rumple. Except for the piston-like motion of his jaw just then engaged in chewing gum, Mel Avrutin and his statue-like pose fit the image of an unbending autocrat. I noted his white shoes when he stepped forward to greet us.

The décor furthered the color scheme. Black-and-white photos graced the gray walls above the black desk and the surrounding gray-metal file cabinets: a formal Mel Avrutin with a smiling President Kennedy; a less formal Mel Avrutin with a beaming Hubert Humphrey; a straight-backed Mel Avrutin with the grinning mayor of Los Angeles. There was even a picture of Avrutin with Teacher and Torres, the two sellouts on the school board who'd undermined our strike. You'd think the executive director of the teachers' union would be too embarrassed to display that one.

In a far corner of the office partially hidden by one of the file cabinets stood a handful of picket signs. "No contract, no work," all the signs read. Without them, you couldn't have distinguished Avrutin's office from any across the city at the Fort. Except that this one belonged to a gum-chewer, which people who worked at the board weren't supposed to be.

Avrutin waved us in and after an exchange of greetings indicated the two black leather chairs opposite his desk.

"Let's cut to the chase, okay?" he said as soon as we were seated. He spoke with a New York accent and left out words and clipped his sentences like a salesman hurrying to complete a deal. "Show me what you got."

Mandy passed him the manila folder containing our work of the night before, and he read her brief but poignant professional history while working his gum. Every so often you could hear it crack. There was no other reaction, and I couldn't tell whether his indifference was a tribute to his lack of interest, his unconcern with the past, or—dare I suggest—his appreciation of the thoroughness of our report.

At last, he put the pages down. Maneuvering the gum from one side of his mouth to the other, he looked at Mandy and asked, "Bottom line, what do you want?"

The question was a homerun pitch, and Mandy answered it with deliberateness and precision: "I want my job back at Cooper."

"Can't promise you that," he said and moved the gum over to where it had started.

"That's it?" I demanded. "That's all you can do for her? I'm her rep, and I expect more from the union."

He ignored me and said to Mandy, "What else?"

"After all this," she said, "I'd like some sort of commitment from the board that assures me I'm entitled to a contract if all goes well throughout this semester—and I'd like it in writing."

"Listen to her," I said. "Why should she have to go through all this nonsense and then have the board forget the deal Thompson made with Woods? Like how they so conveniently forgot to keep her at the same school for a year."

"Okay," the executive director grinned at me, "okay." To Mandy, he said, "You got it." With a chuckle, he nodded at the folder—at her professional life, really. "Tell me," he said, "ever get the feeling someone's out to get you?"

"Who?" I cut in, "the board or the union?"

Avrutin stopped smiling and pointed a finger at me. "Hold on," he said. "I'm on your side here. You want to keep it that way."

Mandy shot me a look to shut me up. She was right. I'd already caused enough grief.

"Thank you for your help," Mandy said to the executive director as she got to her feet and collected her papers.

Avrutin rose behind his desk. "I'll talk to Thompson on Monday and call you later that afternoon with the details."

"I hope so," I told him. "But we've heard that kind of thing before from other people in this union."

Mandy aimed another scowl in my direction while the executive director said, "Well, you haven't heard it from Mel Avrutin. When I say I'll get back to somebody, I get back to them. Don't go holding me accountable for what other people do."

Mandy grabbed my arm and steered me towards the door.

🎓

I have to say this about the union's executive director: The man kept his word. On Monday he called Mandy to confirm that although he couldn't arrange for her to be returned to Cooper, he could state with certainty that a letter was in the mail guaranteeing a contract once she successfully completed her current semester at Paine.

Avrutin's promise certainly sounded reassuring, and yet fulfilling her part of the deal remained a challenge for Mandy. Facing five classes of junior high school kids every day is stressful enough—especially when you're the one they blame for ousting their favorite teacher. But it's that much worse when they're joined by a group of super-critical adults who hold your job in the balance.

Mandy faced a parade of observers—ten visits to her classroom in the next two weeks. Not only did the pink-slippered principal show up, but so did the rest of Paine's administrative staff, including a stern-faced vice-principal and the eye-patch-wearing head counselor. Sitting in the back of the room with pen and paper at the ready, they all took their best shots at Mandy, handing her notes on their way out the door that dealt with everything about her teaching from the number of quizzes she gave to the length of her hair.

Jo Purcell, the social studies chair, also made an appearance. While she seemed sympathetic, she nonetheless wanted to see Mandy's lesson plans three weeks in advance, well beyond the standard one-week request. The department chair explained that she needed enough time not only to examine the logistics of the lessons but also to grant prior approval for the subject-matter Mandy intended to teach. Clearly, the administrators at Paine didn't want any agitators riling their student body.

Its punitive nature aside, a three-week timeline is impractical, especially in a junior high school. Assemblies pop up, last-minute field trips materialize, impromptu sports events occur—all destined to disrupt a teacher's long-range plans. Naturally, it fell to Mandy to make the adjustments.

So grueling was it all that I could now understand why more and more frequently Mandy would come home and spend the remainder of the afternoon at her easel instead of grading papers. Too often, it wasn't until late into the night that she completed her schoolwork.

🎓

Yet even as the scrutiny continued, a most peculiar development occurred in the middle of her fifth week at Paine—Mandy's first out-of-class exchange with the principal.

"It was bizarre," Mandy told me. "Mrs. Flowers stopped me in the hallway as I was going to the cafeteria. I figured she wanted to talk about her last observation."

"No 'come-into-my-office' like Laws?" I asked. "Or even just meeting in your classroom?"

"Nope. With a crooked finger, she beckoned me towards her. She's pretty short in those pink slippers, and I had to bend over to hear her. And even then, she looked up and down the hallway to make sure nobody was close enough to listen in."

"So, what's the great mystery?"

"She checked both ways again, and then she said to me in a squeaky voice—almost a croak, really—like in a scary movie: 'You know, my dear—' (Mandy did her best to imitate the old woman) — 'the board wants me to ice you.'"

"Ice?" I exclaimed. To me, it sounded more like "kill." "What's that supposed to mean?"

Mandy laughed at my look of horror. "I interpreted it as get-me-fired."

"That's bad enough," I said, once again unable to understand Mandy's upbeat attitude. "You're supposed to be getting a contract after this semester, not fired."

"Let me finish, Art. Mrs. Flowers wasn't done. She told me that she didn't care what they wanted downtown. She told me she was going to retire soon so they didn't have a hold over her anymore. If I did a good job, she said she'd give me a fair shake."

Suddenly, I saw things in a new light, maybe here was another principal, like Mrs. Sanchez at Cooper, who displayed a sense of decency.

"Wait a minute," I said, grabbing Mandy's hands, "what if all those visits to your classroom weren't meant to trap you? What if they're Mrs. Flowers' way of protecting you—so when she tells her bosses how great you are, she'll have the evidence to back it up?"

Despite such hopes, Mandy's semester continued to limp along with uncertainty. On the plus side, just as Mel Avrutin had promised, she received a letter from Superintendent Thompson offering her a new contract contingent upon her successfully completing two semesters of teaching regardless of the number of schools. And yet while the frequency of observations lessened, the administrators—Mrs. Flowers in particular—kept up their habitual visits to Mandy's classroom.

I don't mean to suggest that Mandy was unhappy at Paine. The interview assignment in her history classes, which turned out to be as big a hit there as it had been at Phillips and Cooper, helped students appreciate the good teacher they had. She even managed to make a few friends—Jo Purcell, though still requiring those lesson plans, actually became a lunch partner. Not even getting underpaid one month—as had happened in April—seemed to bother her.

To me, missing a part of one's salary, however small the discrepancy, is a big deal; but all Mandy said was, "Mrs. Flowers told me she'd clear it up." With renewed confidence, Mandy added, "Not to worry."

One afternoon in mid-May, I heard Mandy's footsteps running up the metal stairs of our apartment. On earlier occasions, the sound heralded trouble. But before I even got the chance to figure out what to be afraid of, Mandy burst into the living room waving a sheet of paper.

"I passed!" she shouted, dropping her purse and books onto the couch. "Meets-or-exceeds in every category."

I sprang from the chair and wrapped my arms around her. In our frantic clutching, the paper she'd been waving—actually, the evaluation form—arced to the floor, coming to rest beneath the coffee table.

Quickly, I broke free and picked it up. How right she was! In addition to all areas of her performance, but especially in the summary box for the entire semester, the longed-for term, "meets or exceeds expectations," had been checked off—recorded proof on an official district form signed by the principal—a historical document, really —that Mandy's "rehab" had succeeded.

"God bless Mrs. Flowers!" Mandy crowed.

I grabbed the Harvey's and filled two sherry glasses while Mandy told me all the great things Mrs. Flowers had written—how Miss Sayer was doing a wonderful job, how outgoing and friendly Miss Sayer was, and how much students enjoyed being in Miss Sayer's class. The principal's final comment summed it all up: "We're extremely happy to have Miss Sayer at Paine."

"To Mrs. Flowers," I said, and we both raised our glasses.

A couple of afternoons later I was seated at the desk in our apartment correcting a set of essays.

I'd graded about half of them when once more I heard footsteps running up the stairs.

"Put down those papers," Mandy said as soon as she came through the door. "I've got a story I have to tell you." She dropped her book bag onto the coffee table, plopped herself down on the couch, and patted the cushion beside her.

"What's up?" I asked as I nestled in next to her.

"Just listen." Her green eyes beamed with excitement. "Mrs. Flowers called me into her office as I was leaving school today. Remember when I got underpaid last month?"

I nodded. "You said she'd take care of it." Maybe Mandy's gotten the money back, I thought. Dinner on her tonight?

"Well, Mrs. Flowers was on the phone talking to somebody at the Fort about it and motioned me to sit down."

"Are you saying that they're not going to pay you?"

"Let me finish—the money's not the thing."

Clearly, I was missing the point.

"So I'm sitting there listening to Mrs. Flowers explain to some bureaucrat how a mix-up had occurred with my paycheck. And in trying to identify me, Mrs. Flowers said, "You know, the one with the boyfriend the principal didn't like."

My gut clenched as the reference suddenly focused on me. "She's talking to whom now?"

"Who knows? Some flunkey at payroll. That's not the point. Maybe I'm dumb—but I wasn't even aware that Mrs. Flowers knew my history with Laws. I mean, I was placed at the school by the board. There was no interview or anything. But it turns out, she knew my story from the start."

"Laws probably got to her."

"Maybe. But here's the thing. If it was so easy to label me like that—you know, 'the one with the boyfriend. . .' –to some nobody at the Fort, then he must know the story too. And if some nobody knows the story, you have to wonder just how many other people downtown know it as well."

"I get it," I said. "You're Amanda Sayer— the one with the boyfriend her principal didn't like. Could they have treated you any worse?"

"The whole sordid story must be common knowledge."

"Must be," I said slowly.

"When Mrs. Flowers hung up, she assured me that the paycheck problem would be straightened out. But by now I was way more interested in just how many different people in the district had heard about my past. So get this, Art—I asked her."

I opened my eyes wide. I loved her directness. "And?"

"Wait," Mandy cautioned, holding up her hand, "it gets better. A big grin suggested she was about to spill a juicy secret. "So, Mrs. Flowers leans forward, and almost in a whisper, she says,"—here Mandy imitated her again—"'Really, my dear, everybody downtown knows about the trouble you had at your first school—how the principal had some sort of vendetta against your boyfriend.'"

I shook my head in disbelief. First, they wanted to "ice" Mandy; now they were connecting Laws to a "vendetta." It sounded like mob-talk to me.

But Mandy wasn't finished. "Mrs. Flowers said, 'Your boyfriend's the union rep at your first school, isn't he?' I told her you are. She said, 'He has tenure, doesn't he?' and I told her you do. 'And he teaches English, a vital field, right?'"

"She got all that down correctly."

"Exactly. What's more, Mrs. Flowers said that now it all made sense—my old principal figured that hurting me—the union rep's girlfriend—would make my boyfriend suffer more than anything he could do to a tenured English teacher."

I stared at Mandy. "It's just like you said—they all knew, and they still let it go on. My God, they really do tolerate this shit. It really is business as usual."

Mandy nodded. "Right—just like I said, 'common knowledge.' When Mrs. Flowers first got my name from Joe Pontiac, she said he called me the girl who got screwed because of her union boyfriend." Mandy pointed her finger at me. "That would be you."

I had nothing to say. To the board, I may have been the "union boyfriend," but to Mandy, I was obviously the "clueless boyfriend." Call me naive, but we'd never been completely sure about the cause of her problems. Sure, Mandy told me that day in the district parking lot how she suspected that I was Laws's real target; but even though I came around to believing her, for the past two years we'd really only been guessing why Laws had been on her case. Now we had corroboration.

I remained silent while Mandy, still pointing her finger at me, waited for a response. When she realized that I had none, she took hold of my hands. "It's what you've wanted, Art. The whole story. The truth."

Finally, I said, "Holy shit." Except that it came out a lot more gently than I had anticipated.

Mandy cupped my chin with her palm and gently turned my face towards hers. "I'm thrilled to get all this out in the open. Maybe now we can put it behind us."

I didn't smile in return. Maybe I was too fixated on my own starring role in the drama.

Mandy knit her brow. "What are you thinking?" she asked. "You look like you're lost in space somewhere."

Slowly but surely, the truth was beginning to dawn on me: ever since I'd become union rep at Phillips, there had been a part of me that must have wanted to be Laws's target. If being disliked by his teachers supposedly proved to him that he had achieved success, then maybe in my case, being victimized by a strong-armed authoritarian validated my own sense of righteousness. "Confirmation is a powerful force," I said at last, "though not necessarily a flattering one."

Mandy shook her head. "I lost my job, got kicked around from school to school, and all you seem to be concerned with is being right. I guess being right's a big deal to you."

"You know me so well," I said.

"We know each other so well," she whispered back, "and that makes all the difference even if—"

I cut her off in mid-speech to complete her sentence. "—even if Laws really was after me."

"That's not what I was going to say." With a sprinkle of laughter, she added: "—even if both of you are egocentric assholes."

In the last week of May, I found a note in my mailbox, a request from Mandy to call her in the Paine social studies office after school. The last time I'd received a message at Phillips from her, she'd been displaced from Cooper. When I reached her on this occasion, however, she sounded very much at ease.

"I've been officially offered a new contract," she said matter-of-factly. "I wanted you to know."

There it was. After all the battles, the phone calls, the crying, the teeth-grinding, the sleepless nights—after all that, Mandy was about to achieve vindication.

"That's great," I said. "Really."

And yet there was silence on the line. It made me think she wasn't telling me everything. "What's wrong? A contract is what you've been after all this time. It's been your goal from the start."

"Of course, it has. But I'm so close now that I have to ask myself whether working for this school district is what I really want. Do I even want to be a teacher anymore—with all the games you have to play to keep your job?"

On the phone as we were, I could only imagine her confusion. "Listen, Mandy, we shouldn't be discussing all this so publicly."

"You're right. The reason I called was to tell you that in spite of my doubts, I'm still going downtown after school today to sign the contract— in Pontiac's office this time around. Given all we've been through, I'd like you to be there too."

Naturally, I agreed.

She said she'd pick me up at Phillips, and then she hung up.

Returning to district headquarters completed Mandy's odyssey. I'd hoped to see her happy at the prospect of receiving her contract, but clearly she wasn't. In fact, the closer we got to the Fort, the more her green eyes narrowed and her jaw tightened.

The third-floor office of Assistant Superintendent Joe Pontiac occupied the same distant corner of school district headquarters as that of Dr. Thompson. Like Thompson's, Pontiac's office consisted of a small, gray waiting room with a door in the rear that led to the administrator's workspace. Mandy informed Pontiac's secretary that she had an appointment regarding Mandy's contract; and the secretary, looking up through thick round glasses, nodded in the direction of the black vinyl couch behind us.

"This entire business," Mandy complained as we sat down, "would be less annoying if I hadn't done it before—though I have to admit it was easier last time. All I had to do was sign my name at a walk-up window."

The secretary, seemingly oblivious to our conversation, picked up a single sheet of light-blue paper from her desk, affixed it to a clipboard, and handed it to Mandy. At the top of the page, I could see the school district's round logo and in large letters the title, "Contract of Employment."

The secretary indicated with her pencil the signature-line at the bottom. It was highlighted in yellow. "Please read this and sign," she said.

"That's it?" Mandy asked, her voice rich with sarcasm. "No trumpets? No cameras?"

Through her thick lenses, the secretary displayed a blank stare. It looked like it had been cultivated. Then she did an about-face, returned to her desk, and resumed typing.

I looked over at the page as Mandy read it. Having signed a similar contract my first year of teaching, I recognized the standard paragraph on professional responsibilities—arriving on time, dressing appropriately, and completing such obvious duties as taking roll, attending meetings, and assigning grades. The contract labeled such actions as "Reasonably Expected"—an "elastic clause," if ever there were one—and agreed to by the union.

Suddenly, Mandy pointed to the bottom of the page. "Look at this, Art—paragraph seven."

Across the room the typing stopped, and the secretary turned in our direction. "That's new," she said, peering over the top of her glasses. I was wrong about her; she'd been listening to our every word.

"'I certify,'" Mandy read aloud, "'that I have not been dismissed or been issued a less-than-satisfactory performance-evaluation while serving as an employee.'"

"It's nothing to worry about," said the secretary. "It was put in as part of the strike settlement. It's strictly routine."

"Maybe for you," Mandy countered.

The secretary's eyebrows arched, and she turned back to her work and resumed typing.

Pontiac had to know that it was the less-than-satisfactory evaluation at Phillips that had been the catalyst for all of Mandy's troubles. Superintendent Thompson may have assured her that she would qualify for a contract after a year of successful service, but neither he nor any other district official had bothered to alert her to this offensive clause, let alone offer a waiver to nullify it.

Mandy's response was breathtakingly simple: "I can't sign this. I'd be lying if I did."

Was there no way out from under the shadow of Vivian Laws? To have climbed back so far only to confront yet another obstacle—in this case, a towering spool of red tape.

The secretary placed her glasses on her desk and stood up. "Wait one moment," she said. "I'll get Superintendent Pontiac." Then she walked the few feet to the door behind her, knocked briskly, and entered.

Described by Mandy as the voice that hummed on the telephone, Joe Pontiac—in reality, a tall, slender, blue-eyed man with neatly-cut graying hair—emerged from his office a few moments later trailed by the secretary. In his pinstriped, navy-blue suit, Pontiac looked as if he should have been conversing with the chairman of some board on Madison Avenue or maybe modeling clothes in *GQ* or *Esquire.*

Mandy started to explain. "I've—"

The superintendent held up his hand, shook his head, and smiled. "Margot has already told me. The satisfactory-performance clause? Not to worry, dear. Forget it. Just sign." He even offered her a silver Cross-pen for the occasion.

"Just sign?" she said. "Agree that I never got a less-than-satisfactory review when I have? Isn't that perjury? Or just more bureaucratic nonsense that means about as much as the previous contract you could take back whenever you felt like it?"

She handed the paper to Pontiac. "I won't sign this."

"My dear," he began—

Mandy cut him off. "I'm not your 'dear.' What I am is a damn good teacher who's been working for two full years in this district and suffering most all of that time. Two years—and I'm only getting credit for one."

"Now, now," said Pontiac.

"Now, now, yourself. If I teach in this district for forty years, I'll still only be credited with thirty-nine. For forty years I'll be constantly reminded of how this school district mistreated me from the very start—all explained away with the dishonest excuse of helping children."

Pontiac raised both hands, palms down, to quiet Mandy, but she would have none of it.

"You want me to sign a contract that claims all my suffering didn't exist—that the almighty requirements had been nothing to worry about from the start."

"I never said—"

"What you are saying, sir, is that the board's rules really aren't important—because people like you can ignore them whenever you find it convenient."

"Now, Miss Sayer—" Pontiac tried again.

But Mandy had saved her best shot till last. "Do you know what, Mr. Pontiac?" she said slowly. "I don't ever want to work for you people again."

I said nothing.

Chapter Twenty-one

Swan Song

As the end of the school year approached, the dramatic release of the so-called "Pentagon Papers," the Defense Department's classified history of America's political and military actions in Vietnam, filled much of our cafeteria talk. Military analyst Daniel Ellsberg had covertly photocopied and released to the press a trove of secret government documents that revealed a much more extensive and brutal American involvement in Southeast Asia than the public had previously been told of. Ellsberg had exposed the corrupt nature of the bureaucracy.

Leave it to Jack to compare Ellsberg's description of the relationship between the government and the citizenry to that of the school board and us. "It was a tribute to the American people," Jack quoted Ellsberg as saying, "that our leaders had to lie to us, but it was no tribute that we could be lied to so easily."

A dissembling school district administration? Its teachers being lied to? I figured Mandy could relate.

Yet if truth be told, in June of '71—with all due respect to Daniel Ellsberg and his important revelations—Jack talked more and more about his own much-anticipated retirement. In fact, the closer we got to the end of the semester, the more animated and detailed he became on the subject. His tufted eyebrows rose and his hands waved whenever he discussed his upcoming travel plans. He and Myrna had finally bought the Winnebago they'd been dreaming of for years.

"Right after school ends," he said, "we're planning to drive clear across the country." He announced this last bit with a broad sweep of both arms.

"We're all so jealous," Betty said. "You'll be going off to look for America—like in the Simon and Garfunkel song."

"That's right," he agreed, not getting the musical reference. "I can hardly wait for the final bell." He then offered an elaborate description of the Grand Canyon, their first intended destination.

By the time Jack started in on Yellowstone, Betty was more than ready to change the subject. "How's Mandy doing?" she asked me.

"The same," I said. "She still plans to go back to school—maybe at UCLA—and become an architect. She's hoping for a scholarship, but if she has to, she'll find some job for a year or two to make enough money for tuition."

"What a loss," Jack said, shaking his head.

I shrugged. "I can't encourage her to stay in this profession any longer—not after all she's been through—not after the way the school district has treated her."

"You know what?" Betty said. "She's a great teacher—she'll be a great architect."

"Yeah," Jack agreed, "a great architect. Unfortunately, the world is full of great professionals who used to be teachers. Over the years I've met my share—lawyers, journalists, even actors—who started out as teachers, then left education forever."

Jack was right. Aside from a love of teaching, there were few rewards to keep people in the profession. The three of us sat quietly contemplating that fact until the bell interrupted and sent us back to our classrooms.

On most campuses in those days, the pupil-free last-day-of-school provided principals the opportunity to show their benevolence. As soon as teachers completed locking down their classrooms for the summer, many a principal allowed their faculty to leave. As might be expected, however, Vivian Laws, kept us in the building till the last bell tolled.

Years before I ever got to Phillips, some teacher must have said loud enough for others to hear, "If we have to stay anyway, let's enjoy ourselves." Thus was born the end-of-the-year luncheon. It was set up in the spacious student cafeteria where there was lots of room. The faculty collected money for food and gifts, and even the administration chipped in. As the senior homemaking teacher on the staff, Corny Whitaker oversaw the proceedings to make certain the event followed the proper rules of etiquette.

The highlight of the luncheon on this occasion was the celebration of Jack's retirement, and there was a sense of ceremony in the room. Having served for so long as the faculty's political leader, Jack was no ordinary teacher. While lots of people disagreed with him over the years, no one doubted his commitment to improving the working conditions at Phillips.

Jack himself had the dubious honor of sitting at the head table with the administrative staff. To his right sat his wife Myrna, a small, gray-headed lady making her first and, as far as I knew, only appearance at a teachers' social function. To his left sat the school's administrators: Norovsky, Steele, Swett, and Laws.

On the white-brick wall behind the principal hung the new Phillips coat of arms. Penelope Martinez's poster-board drawing of the blue-and-red shield had been recently transformed into an eight-foot-by-ten-foot wall-hanging made of satin. Normally, the thing graced the mid-level landing of the school's central staircase, but on special occasions, like a retirement celebration, Laws allowed it to be moved.

Following a lunch of deli-food, Don Frick, whose wry sense of humor—certainly not his politics—had earned him the job of master-of-ceremonies, called the assemblage to order. The people who were still eating finished up and bussed their dishes while others poured themselves a final cup of coffee.

Amplified as it was through Laws's sound system, Frick's voice boomed to every corner of the cafeteria. "I know you've all been wondering," he began, "so let me tell you about retirement—at least, retirement according to Jack Pointer. One afternoon you get invited downtown by the board to their 'Retirement Tea.' It sounds pretty classy— 'tea and crumpets.'" He got a few laughs pronouncing the words with an exaggerated British accent and raising his little finger as if he were holding a dainty teacup.

"After the cake—the same cake we get here in the cafe, by the way—they have a little ceremony. They give each retiring teacher a gift—a small, potted plant. First, they call the teachers who've hung in for thirty years to come up and get theirs. Then, the thirty-fivers. Finally, they call up the crazies—Jack's group—the people who've taught over forty years. That's when they discovered they'd run out of plants."

Explosions of laughter rocked the room. "I kid you not," Frick said, raising his right hand as if swearing to tell the truth. "They actually ran out of plants—Jack told me the story himself. You can't make this stuff up."

Jack nodded in confirmation. Myrna reacted with a giggle that bubbled into a loud laugh, and she clapped her hands together.

When the laughter subsided, Frick leaned over and lifted up a large, white canvas bag. From inside it, he pulled out a clay pot containing a large bromeliad, one of those green, leafy succulents with a red rosette in the center. He displayed the plant for everyone to see and then summoned the guest of honor to the microphone.

Jack stood, adjusted his tie, and straightened the lapels of his blue suit. Then he made his way to the podium.

"Jack," the woodshop teacher said as he handed over the bromeliad, "in honor of your forty years of teaching, I present to you on behalf of the Phillips faculty a token of appreciation for all your hard work—the same token of deeply felt appreciation, I might add, that the school board ran out of."

A wave of applause broke across the room, and then Jeremy Goodman, who was sitting with Betty, stood up. He'd been subbing elsewhere that day, but to honor Jack, he made the point of returning to Phillips for the luncheon. Raising his fist, Jeremy began the chant, the political cry, which most people had been too intimidated to utter in the days when Jack was still building rep: "Union Jack. Union Jack. Union Jack."

Within seconds, everyone in the room—teachers like me, who considered the man a mentor;

teachers who hardly knew him; and even teachers who had no use for him—stood and joined in the clapping and shouting. "Union Jack" we chanted over and over again. Even Vivian Laws and the other administrators joined the applause—if not the chanting.

Everyone appreciates retiring. It is, after all, the goal of all jobholders, an event that cuts across political lines—a common denominator, an equalizer.

When the cheering finally ebbed and people sat down, Frick handed Jack the microphone and returned to his seat. The former union rep rubbed his hand across his bald head, thanked Don Frick for the bromeliad, and looking around the cafeteria said, "Thank you all. In my new spare time, I can plant this thing in my backyard—although I'm not yet ready to spend all of my retirement cultivating my garden."

"Just remember I want the bag back," Frick called out from his seat.

Amid a few chuckles, Jack held up the bromeliad. "Seriously," he said, "this plant will always remind me of my fond memories of teaching. I could have gone a few more years, but I decided to quit while the good memories still outweigh the bad."

Jack paused and, placing the potted plant on the white tablecloth in front of him, stared at it for a moment. Then he began his farewell address.

"Teaching is a noble profession—who among us hasn't heard that?"

"Right," people were saying, some more sarcastically than others.

"Well," he said, "after forty years of doing it, I'm here to tell you that the job is all that they say it is—as long you're truly teaching. As long as it's you and the kids."

"Amen, brother," somebody said.

Jack smiled. "Whatever your subject— English, math, social studies—what can be more exciting than hearing those wonderful words, 'Oh, I get it,' as your students light up with the joy of discovery?"

Jack looked at me before scanning the rest of the crowd. Throughout the cafeteria, teachers were nodding.

"I'm happy to see that there are always new generations of educators—however small their number—who are eager to pick up the torch that President Kennedy spoke of—even though we all realize the struggles they'll have to face." He looked in my direction again—well aware, I'm certain, how much his words applied to Mandy.

Then he looked to his left, where the administrators sat. "My disagreements with the people who run the school are countless and well-known, even though—more often than not—I've been on the losing side."

Laws may have been nodding and chuckling silently, but I knew it was really the kids, not Jack, who'd lost.

"Principals like to point out that we're all in this business together," Jack said. "Well, let me tell you what I've come to learn during my career. If something good is going to happen to kids at school, it's going to happen in your classrooms."

The audience was still. I wished Mandy could have been there.

"I don't want to overstay my welcome up here," Jack said. "I mean, it's been forty years already." Once more, he held up the potted plant, this time pretending to offer a toast. "To those of you who remain behind—I salute you. I wish you all the very best of luck." With one of his trademark winks, he added, "You're going to need it."

The cafeteria remained silent while Jack, carrying his plant in one arm, moved down the line of administrators and shook hands with each one. Then, as he slowly walked back to his seat at the far end of the table to join Myrna, the faculty rose as one and applauded. Once more the cry of "Union Jack" filled the air.

At Paine, Mandy hadn't made public her plans to leave teaching. And no one saluted her service.

Following the luncheon, I returned to my classroom. I'd already put away most of my teaching paraphernalia; but in the time remaining before we could check out, I had a couple of last-minute house-keeping chores to attend to. I'd taken down my posters and charts, but I needed to strip the bulletin boards of the now-faded yellow construction paper and put away the few books still out, so the shelves and the rest of the room could be properly cleaned during the summer.

I'd cleared the boards and was moving a final pile of dictionaries from my desktop into the cabinet behind it when Jeremy Goodman appeared at the door.

"Hey, man," he asked, "what's up?"

"Sorry I missed you in the cafe," I said as I stacked the dictionaries on the bottom shelf of the cabinet, "but I had to finish in here. I'm due to meet Jack at 3:00 in the office to say good-bye."

Jeremy slipped his hands into his pockets and took a few steps forward. "No sweat. I just came in because I wanted to tell you that I landed a permanent job at Whitman next September."

"At Whitman?" I said, turning to look at him. "That's terrific, really. Congratulations." It was indeed a great move for the guy, but a flash of jealousy shot through me. Whitman was the closest high school to Phillips, and most of our kids went on to school there. In fact, it was where I had always hoped to end up teaching.

293

"Thanks," Jeremy said. "I'm pretty jazzed about it. I've been subbing over there most of the year, and they asked me to come back full time."

"Whitman's a great school. I wouldn't mind transferring there myself."

"Hey, mate, you don't think I know that? Betty tells me all the time how you guys are always taking about teaching in high school."

"True enough," I said, resuming my work with the books.

"That's why I came in here. Did you think I just wanted to brag or something? Shit, I wanted to tell you that the English chair at Whitman said they'd love to have you there."

With a dictionary in hand, I turned around again and stared at Jeremy. "Really?"

"Really, man. He said they've heard nothing but good things about Mr. Malamud from the Phillips kids who go there. In fact, the department chair said he'd called the old man last month to see if you were available next year. To be honest, it was only after they found out that you weren't that they offered me the job."

"You're kidding, right? Of course, I was available—still am."

"Not according to Laws. The asshole doesn't want to let you go. I figured he wouldn't even tell you that Whitman asked. That's why I came in here—to fill you in."

The more Jeremy talked, the angrier I got.

"You know," Jeremy said, flashing a half-hearted smile, "even if the old man won't release you, it's still quite a compliment to hear that a high school is interested. In a way, it's also kind of a compliment to discover that you're so great at bugging Laws that he wants to keep you here against your will."

"Shit!" I shouted and smashed the dictionary down on my desk.

Jeremy jumped back in surprise.

"Some fucking compliment," I said. "Especially when he knows I'd like nothing better than to get away from him—and transfer to a high school no less."

I shouldn't have been shocked, not once we'd learned how badly Laws had treated Mandy because of me. But this Whitman story—the fact that Laws had ignored his chance to dump me, to rid himself of me—pissed me off all the more.

"Well," Jeremy said, "that's all I had to tell you. In some sick way, it's sort of like good news— being wanted by Whitman, I mean. Anyhow, have a great summer." He offered a brief wave. "Later, man," he said and strolled out the door.

In frustration, I shoved the remaining dictionaries into the cabinet and slammed the door shut. I took one final look around, walked out into the hallway, and locked up my room. Then I marched down the stairs, past the blank wall where the new Phillips coat-of-arms usually hung, and into the main office.

Abe Norovsky had the job of collecting our roll books and school keys before we left for the summer. Harry Barnes was handing over his roll book when I arrived.

"Hey, Harry." I greeted him with a strong handshake and pat on the back. "Have a really great vacation."

He turned with a quizzical look. "Yeah, you too," he said.

My enthusiastic come-on obviously puzzled him, but whenever I saw the guy, I felt guilty for having given his name to Laws when Mandy's fate had remained unclear. Well, at least the guy hadn't lost his position.

Barnes turned back to Norovsky and handed him his keys. While the head counselor was filing them away, I stared across the room once more at the portrait of David Graham Phillips. A writer I should learn more about, I was thinking when I felt Jack's bear-like arm drape across my shoulder.

"He was quite a character," the English teacher said, following my gaze back to Phillips' picture. "His novels criticized our political system, and he wrote articles that attacked Washington politicians. He accused senators of treason for not representing the people. He was somebody not afraid to speak truth to power."

"Kind of like Ellsberg," I said.

"Kind of," Jack agreed. "Phillips was the first journalist to be called a muckraker."

"No kidding. What happened to him?"

It was Harry Barnes, the history teacher, who answered. "Murdered," he said as he walked off. "Shot dead by a madman."

I looked back with greater respect at the piercing eyes in the portrait. Then I turned my keys and roll book over to Norovsky.

Before it was Jack's turn at the counter, we hugged each other.

"Keep in touch," he said. "I'd call you, but I'd just ask how school was and be afraid you'd tell me."

When I got home, Mrs. Gross was watering the apple tree and nodded at me as I walked past. I smiled back. It was the start of summer vacation. As I mounted the metal stairs, however, I found myself pondering the implications of what Jeremy Goodman had revealed. Mandy had quit; Jack had retired; Jeremy was off to Whitman. I could only wonder when it would be my turn to move on.

Mandy had beaten me home; and as I entered the apartment, I heard the soft sounds of Joan Baez playing on the stereo. The school year had officially ended; and Mandy, the now former-teacher, was already at work at her easel.

On this occasion she had drawn the apple tree that stood just outside the apartment. The metal stairs occupied the background, and she'd even included the mailbox that had figured so prominently in her saga. But it was the tree that dominated the work—in particular, her interpretation of it. For in Mandy's vision the tree had no apples; she had, in fact, reduced it to a skeletal silhouette.

There was sadness in the drawing, but Mandy's green eyes danced with life. And there was something else that caught my attention. It took me a moment to recognize the change, but then I realized—she had cut her hair, her magnificent, long red hair.

"What—what happened?" I asked in surprise.

"I'm starting a new life; I figure I should have a new look." She ran her fingers through her bob. "I had it chopped off right after school and donated it all to charity. What do you think?"

I answered her with a broad smile.

Epilogue

*I*t wasn't until a Saturday evening two years later that I realized this story had finally reached an appropriate conclusion. Life had mellowed since school ended back in June of 1971. American combat troops had left Vietnam, and the discovery that Richard Nixon had taped conversations in the Oval Office threatened his presidency. Mandy was studying architecture at UCLA, and I was still teaching at Phillips while dreaming of Whitman.

On a Saturday night in late July, we'd finished dinner at Canter's and decided to walk down to the Fairfax Theater on Beverly to see some film—I think *Chinatown* was playing at the time. I hadn't been to the Fairfax in many years, but it was still the same old place inside with those tall, yellow art-deco lights on the sidewalls that I remembered from the Saturday matinees I'd gone to as a kid.

Mandy and I had just bought our tickets at the old-fashioned ticket booth when we noticed an elderly Black couple slowly exiting the lobby. The balding man walked with a cane, and the woman wore her gray hair pulled back in a ponytail like a much younger lady. What most caught my eye, however, was her shuffling feet. You couldn't miss those fluffy, pink bedroom slippers.

"Oh my God," Mandy whispered more to herself than to me, "it's Mrs. Flowers, my principal at Paine."

Though I had heard the stories, I had never met the woman; and Mandy, taking my arm, escorted me towards the couple. As soon as Mrs. Flowers saw Mandy, the principal grabbed her, and the two of them hugged like long-lost friends. It was only after they'd let go that Mrs. Flowers turned in my direction. She looked me over for an uncomfortably long time and finally paused to moisten her lips before she spoke.

"Well, my dear," the old woman said to Mandy in a scratchy voice, "I certainly hope he was worth it."

THE END